LOVERS' BREAKFAST

Zack jumped out of bed and sat down at the motel's small rickety table. Paula put his steaming breakfast before him and stood back to watch him attack it. Suddenly their eyes caught and she kissed him.

Zack put down his fork and said slowly, "Paula, I never try to fool anybody about who I am, what I want...so if even at the back of your—"

"I know who you are and what you want," Paula said quickly. Zack looked at her steadily.

"What do *you* want, Paula? What do you really want?"

"To have a good time with you until you have to go," she answered softly.

"That's it?"

"Yes." Paula nodded and turned away so he couldn't see how much she was lying.

AN OFFICER AND A GENTLEMAN

STEVEN PHILLIP SMITH

FROM THE SCREENPLAY WRITTEN BY DOUGLAS DAY STEWART

AVON
PUBLISHERS OF BARD, CAMELOT, DISCUS AND FLARE BOOKS

AN OFFICER AND A GENTLEMAN

Prologue

Zack Mayo left Norfolk, Virginia, a little after his thirteenth birthday, and although his circumstances were less than auspicious—his mother was dead, his grandparents were incapacitated by age, and his only aunt was a hopeless drunk—the day of his departure was one of the happiest of his life. Mr. Fowler from the state school had driven him to the bus depot through a cold rain, admonishing Zack to "do the school proud" at his new home overseas. Zack nodded and smiled, and at the depot he nodded and smiled again, even shaking Mr. Fowler's hand after the old bastard had given him the ticket to D.C., two airplane tickets, a comic book, a candy bar, and a ten-dollar bill.

Maybe it's all a trick, Zack thought, unable to believe that they were actually letting him go. After he boarded the bus he kept expecting Fowler or some other school official to come on and grab him and drag him back to the cold and stinky orphans' home. Once the bus was on its way he kept looking out the window in anticipation of the patrol car that would terminate his brief experience of freedom. But no one came to foil his escape, and in six hours he began the first airplane ride of his life. By the time the plane touched down in California he had decided to become a pilot.

He had a two-hour layover in San Francisco. He went immediately to the coffee shop and wolfed down a hamburger, French fries, a Coke, and a chocolate milk shake, then he bought a couple of Baby Ruth bars to munch on while he watched the gigantic airplanes take off and land. He could imagine nothing better in life than to sit behind the controls of one of these gigantic flying machines, going from place to place at amazing speeds with no one to tell him what to do. He shook his head with the thought of what it must take to become a pilot. They were probably some kind of supermen, chosen for their super powers that people like Zack did not possess. He went back to the coffee shop for another hamburger and Coke, then walked slowly to his boarding gate, convinced that he would never have what it took to fly a plane. He could not even understand how the things stayed up in the air.

On the flight to Manila he finally found the courage to ask the stewardess, who had been pampering him, if he could see the place where the pilots sat. She explained that it was against regulations for passengers to go into the cockpit, but since it was night and most everyone was asleep, she let Zack follow her up the aisle and stand in the doorway when she opened it to take the crew some coffee. The pilot turned around to eyeball the youngster (Zack had fallen into a trance looking at all the dials and switches), decided that he was not a terrorist hijacker, and allowed him to enter the cockpit. When Zack came out he knew that he too would become a pilot. He would have to study hard in school, go to college, and probably spend some time in the military service, as the pilot had, learning how to fly. Those were all things he thought he could do. He truly hated school, but maybe it would be better if he knew he could put it to some use. Both the pilot and his partner had seemed like pretty ordinary guys. Zack went back to his seat and fell asleep, dreaming of flight.

The stewardess shook him awake ten minutes before the airplane was to land in Manila. His dreams of a career in the skies were quickly replaced by a new anxiety: he was about to meet his father for the first time. He pushed a piece of gum into his mouth, then pulled a tattered photo strip from his pocket. The photos were fourteen years old, the kind that came four-for-a-quarter in the arcades of roving carnivals, and each one showed Zack's mother (looking so much younger than he'd ever seen her) in the arms of a handsome sailor. Zack wondered what his father would be like, what this new life in the Philippines would be all about, then comforted himself with the thought that whoever his father was or whatever his life would be like, it could be no worse than what he had left behind him. Besides, he had no one else to turn to, and he had nowhere to go.

The stewardess kissed him good-bye, then Zack found himself descending the ramp to the ground, his little valise, containing all that he owned, in one hand, the photo strip in the other. He was nearly to the bottom before he had picked out the sailor in the group of people waiting to greet the passengers. Zack was surprised that the man didn't look much older than he did in the picture. Could this really be his father?

The man came forward and gave him a nervous smile. "You Zack?"

Zack nodded. "Yes, sir."

"I figured you were my boy when I saw the stewardess kiss you." The man took his valise and shook his hand. "I'm Byron. Nice to meet you."

"Yes, sir."

Byron nodded toward the terminal. "C'mon. Let's go get your luggage."

"That's all I have," Zack said.

Byron slapped him on the back. "Travelin' light, huh? Well, that's my motto too. Move fast and travel light. That's a good way not to get bogged down."

"Yes, sir."

"You hungry?"

"No, sir."

"Well, let's get on the road to Olongapo then. You might as well make your acquaintance with the armpit of the Orient. I hope you won't regret comin' here."

"I won't," Zack said. After the glory of the plane ride he was willing to endure anything.

They caught a little bus—a jeepney, his father called it—and left the airport for Olongapo. Zack was both frightened and excited by the super-chromed, ornately decorated vehicle—he'd never seen decorations on a bus in his life—and also by the strange mixture of small Oriental people jabbering in a foreign tongue. Some of the Filipinos wore suits and ties, others were dressed in the rough attire of farmers. One old woman even carried a cage on her lap in which a chicken squawked and fluttered about.

Whenever he looked at his father he found Byron staring at him in the strangest way. Zack would give him a little smile, then turn back to the passing scenery. After a while Byron leaned over and gave him a little tap on the shoulder. "Hey, kid, why don't you take off that coat. This is the Philippines. You could probably even throw it away."

As Byron helped him out of the coat, Zack realized how hot he was. His clothes were soaked with sweat.

"I reckon it's a long way from Norfolk, hey, kid?" Byron said.

Zack nodded. "I don't care. It can't be far enough."

The jeepney stopped, and a couple of farmers got off. They rode on in silence for a while, then Byron touched Zack's shoulder again. "I was sorry to hear about your mom, Zack. That was pretty rough."

Zack nodded again. He was going to try to put it behind him. Just deal with his new life.

"I would've returned your call sooner," Byron said. "But I was out at sea."

"I was calling for four months," Zack said, feeling an irritation with his father for the first time.

Byron shrugged. "Well, that's how long I was out at sea."

The jeepney stopped again, and the rest of the passengers got out. At the side of the road was a sign that said *U.S. Naval Facility, Subic Bay...12 Miles.*

"Home sweet home," Byron said.

Zack thought he had seen it all on the cheap streets of Norfolk where the sailors spent their liberties getting drunk and going to the fleabag hotels with the whores. (He wasn't too young to know what they were either—he'd had plenty of fights with guys who had suggested that that was how his mother used to make her living.) At least in Norfolk there had been some pretense of keeping things under cover. In Olongapo it hung out all over. The long, rain-rutted street seemed to consist of nothing but gaudy bars and rattan-walled whorehouses. Drunken sailors leaned out of careening jeepneys, bellowing to their companions or to whores or just for the sake of bellowing.

"Them's beenie boys," Byron said, pointing to a pair of especially small Filipinos dressed up as exquisite young girls.

Zack stared at them for a moment, then gave his father a curious look. He'd heard about queers in Norfolk—some of his older friends had even rolled a couple of them—but he'd never seen anything like this.

Byron shrugged. "Sailors are like everyone else. Some of 'em got weird tastes. Not me, though." Byron whistled to a pair of whores lounging in the entrance to a bar called California Dreamin'. Both girls were dressed in nipple-showing tank tops, and one of them waved at Byron while the other licked her lips. Byron elbowed Zack. "I've always had a weakness for the ladies, Zackie."

Zack guessed that his mother could have testified to that.

"I suppose you've still got your cherry," Byron said.

Zack looked away, feeling his face redden.

"Aw, hell, kid. It's okay." Byron slid his arm around his son. "We'll take care of that right quick."

The jeepney pulled up in front of a bar, The Hoosiers Haven, and Byron jumped out. "This is it, kid. This is where I hang my hat."

Zack looked at the bar and shook his head. It was quite possibly the raunchiest one on the block. Inside, Byron was greeted heartily by the old Filipino behind the bar, and a few of the girls waved to him too. Several sailors were making out with the bar girls, and as they left the room Zack saw one woman slide her hand down the front of a sailor's pants. Byron vaulted two drunks sprawled in the stairwell, then turned around to help Zack over them. He gave his son a sheepish smile. "If I was in port more, I'd rent a better place, but this works out okay."

Zack nodded and followed his father up the stairs. He guessed he *had* come halfway around the world. A slightly stale smell hung in the upstairs hallway, but Byron breezed through it as though it were nothing. He unlocked a door and pushed it open, then just stood there shaking his head.

Zack peered around the corner to see two women lying on the big bed, each wearing just a bra and a very' small pair of panties. He couldn't take his eyes off them.

"What the hell?" Byron said. "I thought you girls were going shopping."

The girls just giggled.

"Well," Byron said, "you're goin' shopping now." He reached in his wallet and drew out some money. "Tiki, Maria, I want you to meet my son, Zack."

"Hi," Zack said as the giggling girls got off the bed and began getting dressed. He wondered if all four of them were going to live here together, if he was going to have to spend the night with one of the women in the little cot on the other side of the room. He didn't know if he could handle it, especially with his father looking on and all.

The girls left, and Byron flopped down in the easy chair by the bed and lit a cigarette. He eyed Zack for a moment, then said, "I guess you can bunk on the cot and go to school on the base."

"Great," Zack said.

"I'm not finished." Byron's face suddenly hardened, and his voice came out cold. "I'll only be in port one week a month, and when I'm here you ain't gonna catch me playin' daddy. That ain't the way I'm built." He puffed on his cigarette and blew a steady stream of smoke at the ceiling.

"I got along without it so far." Zack stared steadily at his father.

Byron snorted. "A tough one, huh? Well, I still think you'd be better off in that state school in Virginia, just like I told you on the phone."

Zack shook his head. "I ain't never goin' back to that school, sir."

Byron stared at the floor. "You got to, kid." He looked up suddenly. "Let me spell it out for you. This is a whorehouse you're livin' in."

"I got the picture."

"And I happen to like my life the way it is, and nobody's gonna make me change it."

Zack bit his lip and looked away, fighting tears. It was just as Nesbitt his buddy had told him it would be. No whoremongering swabby was going to give a shit for him. He was going to have to look out for himself. He bent over and picked up his valise, then shot Byron a look. "I don't care about your life, and I sure as hell don't want to change it. I just ain't going back to that school. You don't want me? Fine. I'll find another place." He walked out the door and headed down the stairwell.

In a moment he heard Byron come out on the landing. Zack did not slow down or look back.

"Hey, kid. Come back."

Zack kept moving.

"Come back here, kid!" Byron yelled.

Zack stopped and turned around and shot him his meanest look. "What for?"

Byron shook his head and gave his son a grudging smile. "Okay, okay. You win."

Zack gave him his best smile. "Thank you, sir." He started up the stairs, then stopped when Byron pointed an accusing finger at him. "Stop calling me sir, for Christ's sake! I ain't no officer. My name is Byron."

Zack smiled at his father again.

It was early afternoon, and the men at the bar were all drunk. A chair on rollers was placed on the bar, and one by one the men would sit in it, be pushed the length of the bar, then fly off toward the floor, most of them jumping out just before the chair hit the hard wood. The whores cheered them on, while the other men wagered on who would stay in his chair the longest before bailing out. Zack sat at the bottom of the stairs, watching with great fascination. He knew by the wing insignias on their chests that the men were fliers. One of Byron's girls walked by, and Zack grabbed her hand. "Who are they, Tiki?"

"Hot shot jet jockeys," she said.

Zack smiled. "That's what I want to be some day."

"They off the carrier," Tiki said. "Very drunk now."

"The carrier's in port?"

Tiki nodded.

"I want to go see it," Zack said.

Tiki pointed at the pilots. "Maybe you grow up like that, little Zackie. Fly mach five, no jive." She tousled his hair as he laughed.

"Maybe," Zack said.

"Maybe what?" Byron stood behind him on the stairs, his seabag over his shoulder.

Zack pointed to the men at the bar. "Maybe I'm gonna end up like them."

Byron shook his head. "A six-pack of San Miguel'd do that for you."

"I mean become a flier."

"Oh, I see." Byron nodded with mock gravity. "Sure, kid."

"I'm serious."

"I'm serious about wanting to be chief of staff, too." Byron took in his surroundings. "But somehow I don't think it's in the cards." He bent down and handed Zack some money. "Put this in your shoe, kid, in case you need it. I'm gonna be gone for a while. Don't go gettin' in no trouble. Tiki and Maria'll look out for you."

"Thanks, Byron." Zack hid the money in his shoe.

"If I don't sink, I'll be seein' you." Byron shook his hand, kissed his two mama-sans goodbye, and strode out of the bar.

Zack watched the drunken airmen for half an hour, then left The Hoosiers Haven to go to the harbor and look at the flattop. As he stopped to look at the trinkets in the window of a curio shop, two boys about his age that he had seen around the bar approached him.

"Hey, *palequero*," one of them said. "You new in the P.I.?"

"Been here about a week."

"Come on," the other one said. "We show you some nice things."

"I don't know," Zack said.

"We can really show you around," the first one said.

His partner nodded. "Nobody knows this shit-hole like us."

The two boys burst out laughing, and after a moment Zack laughed too. In a way he trusted them. They reminded him of his buddies in the orphans' home. "Okay, but just for a little while. I want to go look at the aircraft carrier."

"No sweaty-dah, man."

"Let's go."

They had walked about fifty feet when both of the boys pushed Zack into a little alley off the main street.

"Hey!" Zack said.

"Hey, yourself, big spender."

"Give us your money."

Zack eyed them both warily. "I ain't got no money."

The first boy reached out and slapped him. "Bullshit. We seen that swabby give it to you."

"He's not..."

"Get it out!" the second boy yelled.

The first one suddenly kicked Zack in the balls. Zack doubled over, then came up and punched the second boy, sending him flying into a wall.

"Stay there," the first boy said to his partner.

Then he gave Zack a mean little smile. "Not bad. But you've still got a lot to learn." The boy moved, and before Zack could raise his hands he had been kicked in the stomach and the face. He spun around once, then took another savage kick to the groin. Zack bent over, fighting his impulse to fall, then something collided with his head and he dropped facedown in the dirt. He could feel them taking off his shoe, but he was unable to move his body to try and stop them. Later, when he stumbled out of the alley, he nearly tripped over a dead dog. He knew he was going to have to learn how to fight, and he was determined that today would be the last day he would ever be beaten.

1

They never change, Zack thought, never. Search the wide world over, and every place that had the Navy nearby was sure to have the same collection of sleazy, noisy bars, fleabag hotels, credit jewelers, and pawnshops. This time it just happened to be in Seattle, Washington. Zack gunned his Triumph motorcycle past the Seven Seas Locker Club, giving the thumbs up to a scuzzy sailor leaning against a brick wall. Zack caught a glimpse of himself in the rearview mirror. Looking pretty scuzzy too. His long mane of jet-black hair was blown back in the wind, and his beard was in need of an hour's combing. Well, he thought, all that hair's gonna be gone in a couple of days. His bright blue cold eyes were still pretty anyway. He searched the buildings for an address, suddenly inundated with memories of the first time he'd met Byron, of his early inspiration to fly, of the whipping he'd taken from the Filipino boys. Almost ten years ago.

He found the address he wanted, did a U-turn in the middle of the street, and parked in front of the dingy hotel. How did Byron go on like this, year after year, without getting worn out? Zack shook his head, pulled his muddy Levi's over his muddy boots, took his duffel bag off the bike, and entered the hotel. Still traveling light. I suppose I am my father's son, he thought as he climbed the stairs.

In the dingy hallway on the second floor he found one door open, through which he saw a weary woman with an ugly child sitting on a battered couch. A sailor's uniform hung over a chair next to a table. The sailor appeared suddenly and shut the door in Zack's face. "Yeah," Zack said, and continued down the hall. He stopped in front of another door, pulled an old postcard from his pocket and consulted it, then pounded with authority on the scarred wood. "Open up!" he bellowed. "Shore patrol. Shore patrol!" He stepped back with a big grin on his face.

In a moment the door swung open, and Byron appeared, fumbling to conceal his nudity beneath a little kimono. In the rumpled bed behind him Zack could see a naked prostitute who couldn't have been even twenty years old. "One of these days, Byron, you're gonna get a heart attack from those young things."

Dumbfounded, Byron stared at his son for a moment, then a warm smile spread across his face. "Zack, you little shit!" he said. "You haven't changed a bit."

Zack nodded toward the whore. "Neither have you, pard!"

The men guffawed, then came together in a macho embrace as though they were old whoring buddies. After a moment, Byron pulled away. "Christ, kid, you look, uh, great."

"You too, Byron. How you feelin'?"

Byron slapped his flat stomach. "Never better." He flung his arm around his son and led him into the room. "Hey, honey, look at this. My son! Isn't he beautiful?"

She nodded. "Hello, Byron's son."

"Name's Zack," he said.

"Caroline," she said.

"Pleased to meet you."

Byron thumped him on the back. "You should've called."

"You were out at sea." He stroked his beard, eyeing his father. "Hey, guess what?"

"You're married?"

"Nope."

"You're on the lam from the law?"

"Sorry, pard. I graduated. I got my goddamn degree."

Byron gave him a long suspicious look. "You're shittin' me."

"You can't shit an old turd, Byron."

"I thought you quit school. Last I heard you were on your way down to Brazil on some construction job or something."

Zack nodded. "I made some money down there too. Then I talked my way into another college, and I did it. I wasn't magna cum laude, but I did okay."

"Jesus Christ," Byron said.

"You should've seen me in my cap and gown."

"Why the fuck didn't you invite me? I would've come."

Zack gave Byron a skeptical look. "You can't bullshit the bullshitter, pard."

"I would have." Byron turned quickly to Caroline. "Hey, honey, get on the phone. Call up that friend of yours, um, Gloria. The one with the big tits. We're gonna celebrate." Byron puffed up with pride. "Hey, did you hear all that? My son's graduated from college."

Caroline nodded, smiled at Zack, then rolled over lazily and picked up the phone.

It wasn't the first time that Zack had partied with his father, but as he slipped deeper and deeper into oblivion, he resolved that it would be the last. He guessed he'd known that when he'd arrived, but was willing to go through it one more time as a sort of cleansing ritual preparatory to his new life. Christ, how could Byron stand it, the broken-record existence of the lifer enlisted man? The two men lay in the bed together, humping away on the prostitutes beneath them, loaded on wine and grass. He really likes this, Zack thought, sneaking a look at his father in mid-stroke. He felt a wave of nausea, then he shuddered with a sad, shabby feeling as he spied the monkeywood carvings that Byron had brought from the Philippines, on the wall. They were palely illuminated by three candles that were stuck in dishes and rested on what passed for a desk.

Later, as the four of them lay side-by-side, Gloria nudged Zack and said, "Hey, you guys putting us on, right? You're not really father and son."

"Right," Byron said. "We're putting you on. What happened to that joint?"

"I think it went out," Caroline said.

Byron leaned over Zack and Gloria and grabbed the ashtray from the table at the side of the bed. *"Ay, palequero,"* he said to his son.

Zack was nearly asleep, but the sight of Byron's leering face revived him again. *"Ay, palequero,"* he replied. "Never *hochi* in the P.I."

Byron laughed. "Wha-chu-say, sailor boy? Short time, long time, only ten dolla."

Byron guffawed, and Zack couldn't help it; he burst into laughter himself. Soon the women caught it, and the last thing Zack remembered from that night was the four of them passing the joint and roaring in the bed.

In the morning he awoke in a tangle of sheets, his head throbbing, his mouth dry, his nose inhaling Gloria's foul breath. He carefully slipped free of her arm and the soiled sheet, got out of bed, and pulled on his shorts. He thought he might vomit as he looked around the room with its overflowing ashtrays, empty wine bottles, and the naked, snoring people in the bed. But he swallowed his disgust and headed for the bathroom. He gobbled three aspirin and was on his second glass of water when Byron reeled in, shoved him aside, and unceremoniously barfed in the toilet. Zack looked at his father in disgust, hearing in Byron's agonized retch an anthem for his entire life. Byron glanced back at him and held out his hand. "What're you lookin' at?"

Zack shook his head.

"Hand me that towel."

Zack did as he was told.

Byron stood up, wiping off his mouth. He reached around Zack and grabbed a bottle of Lavoris out of the medicine cabinet. "Here's to ya." He toasted his son, took a swig, gargled, and spit the red, foamy liquid into the toilet. "So long, night." Byron flushed, then elbowed his son. "Hey, that was pretty great, wasn't it?"

Zack shrugged.

"I know," Byron said. "Nothin' like that night with them three stewardesses in Manila, but pretty fucking nice all the same."

"I reckon." Zack took a swig of mouthwash too.

"Now what?" Byron asked.

"What do you mean?"

"I mean, what are you gonna do? I never did ask you why you were in Seattle."

Zack grinned at himself in the mirror. "Get ready, pard. This one's gonna blow you away."

Byron snorted. "Zackie, nothing you do will ever surprise me. Not after some of the shit you've pulled."

"I joined the Navy." Zack stroked his beard.

"You what? Jesus Christ..." Byron lowered the seat and sat down on the toilet.

Zack laughed. "Figured that'd get you."

"You? In the Navy? I don't believe it."

"Believe it, pard. I'm on my way over to this officer school in Port Rainier."

Byron stared at the floor. "Officer school," he muttered. "What the hell for?"

"To fly jets. To be the fastest motherfucker in the world. You gotta come and visit me, Byron. It's only a couple hours away."

"I know where it is." Byron stared up at him. "Who gave you this goddamn idea?"

"It started a long time ago."

Byron gave a little laugh. "I don't...Jesus Christ! You in the Navy? And an officer? Gimme a goddamn break. That's like me saying I'm running for fucking president."

Zack felt himself reddening. "It ain't that bad," he said feebly.

"Shit! Look at yourself." Byron pointed at his arm. "I hate to tell you, man, but officers don't have tattoos!" His laughter gave way to a great phlegmy cough, and after a moment he stood up to spit in the toilet.

"Look, pard," Zack said. "I'll be seeing you." He walked into the room and began getting dressed.

Byron followed him in, wiping his mouth on the back of his hand. "Hey, kid, don't be pissed. I'm on your side. I just don't want you to do something you'll regret."

"I won't regret it." Zack pulled on his boots. "I'm gonna make something of myself."

"Aw, Jesus, Zack. You gotta give six years to the Navy if you want to fly. That's six years with the most uptight assholes God put on this earth. Officers ain't like you and me, man. It's another breed altogether."

Zack hoped that that was true. "What's the matter, Chief? You afraid you'll have to salute me or something?"

"Fuck no!" Byron roared. The girls were awake now and staring at the two men. "Why would I care about something as dumb as that?"

"I don't know. That's just how it sounded." Zack eyed his father. "Well, I'll be seeing you." He shouldered his duffel bag, walked to the door and into the hallway.

Byron followed him. "Hey, what'd you want?" he yelled from the doorway. "A lot of fatherly bullshit? A big pat on the back?"

Zack stopped, turned around, and grinned. "From you, pard? Never *hochi*." He turned and started to leave, then stopped and faced his father once again. "Hey, thanks for the graduation present." He continued down the hall. As he started down the stairs he heard his father call, "Hey, Zackie, don't go away mad."

"I'm just goin' away," Zack muttered.

He didn't go far. He gunned the Triumph through the cool morning air for about an hour, blowing the cobwebs out of his head, then stopped at a Holiday Inn and ate a huge breakfast in the coffee shop. He wasn't through with his father; he knew he'd see Byron again, maybe even before he was finished with his training. But he was through with being his father's buddy, especially his whoring buddy. Too goddamn low-life. And lowlifes always stayed the same, living in the same dreary places, getting drunk, grasping for happiness, ending up with a toilet full of puke and a hangover. No way was Zack Mayo going to end up like that. He'd come close so many times, flunking out of one school, getting kicked out of another for his wild behavior. But he kept coming back, always driven by his dreams of being a pilot, and he was too close to blow it now. A few months of training and he'd be on his way to flight school. The kind of people he'd be associating with didn't go out chasing pussy with their fathers. No, he was on his way to becoming an officer and a gentleman.

He rented a room and took a nap, and that afternoon he did a half-hour's worth of calisthenics, then went out and ran five miles. He was in excellent shape, but he wanted to sweat out all the previous night's booze and dope, and he wanted to be ready for anything when the drill instructors took over his life tomorrow. They were going to be tough, he thought later as he trimmed his beard and shaved the stubble. And they'd try to break him at every opportunity. Well, he'd been around the military long enough to know that it was all a big game, that whatever happened, he couldn't take it personally. That was the key to survival. The D.I.'s were looking for weakness, and as far as Zack could see, he didn't have any, at least any that would prevent him from becoming a flier. He wasn't a real genius when it came to math and science, but he was quick—real swift when he had to be. He reckoned that was more important for flying jets. Anyway, he had to make it. He'd come too far not to.

2

In the morning he exercised and shaved again, but he made no effort to conceal the length of his hair. It wouldn't hurt to be known as something of a rebel. But not that much of one, he thought, carefully covering his tattoo with a couple of Band-Aids. He guessed that Byron was right on that score—the only officers he'd ever seen with tattoos were the ones who'd come up through the ranks. Zack shrugged; in a way, he was coming up through the ranks too. He put his shaving kit into his duffel bag, which contained two changes of clothes and a small box of memorabilia—he wasn't exactly weighed down with good memories—checked himself in the mirror for the last time, shouldered the bag, and strode out of the room.

As he cruised through the gate of the sprawling air station, he saw a sign that read *Through*

These Gates Pass the Future of Naval Aviation.
"Right here, brother," he said out loud. He almost ran off the road near the airfield as he watched a line of aircraft. "Steady, boy," he said to himself, stopping at an intersection to let a bedraggled class of candidates double-time past him. On a huge parade ground on the other side of the road, two other classes of candidates drilled with rifles. Fun and games, Zack thought. The thought of the drill didn't scare him at all. He'd had some R.O.T.C., and he'd seen plenty of it in the Philippines. Just don't take it personally, he thought.

An F-14 "Tomcat" jet fighter sat like a sculpture in front of the administration building. Zack parked his motorcycle beside it and dismounted slowly while a lieutenant in aviator sunglasses stared at him. After a moment the man said, "What can I do for you, son?"

"I'm here for Aviation Officer Candidate School," Zack said proudly.

The lieutenant pointed over Zack's shoulder. "You can join those other civilian types beneath that tree."

Zack looked back at his future classmates, then smiled at the lieutenant. "Thank you, sir," he said.

The lieutenant shook his head. "You won't be thankin' me after you meet Foley."

"I'll bet." Halfway to the tree, he stopped to watch a girl get out of an Audi 5000, kiss an older man and woman good-bye, and get her directions from the lieutenant. She had the slim, athletic body of a runner, and her pretty face did not have the slightest hint of makeup. Zack smiled at her as she approached him. "The future of naval aviation," he said.

"Count on it," the girl said. "I hope it doesn't rest with you."

"We'll just have to see about that," Zack said.

"Yes, we will." She walked past him.

He turned to see most of the other thirty men beneath the tree ogling the new arrival who quickly joined the five women off to the side. Zack approached a tall, almost hulking candidate. "I think I'm gonna like this modern Navy," Zack said.

The man gave him a big, open grin and nodded enthusiastically. "Yeah," he said. "All right." The man's expression suddenly changed, and Zack turned as several other candidates began nervously shuffling about.

The tall, black Marine staff sergeant strode smartly toward them, his face all business. He came to a heel-clapping halt by a white line on the pavement ten feet in front of them, eyeing the group with contempt from beneath the brim of his Smokey-the-Bear hat. His uniform was perfectly pressed, his boots perfectly polished, his belt buckle perfectly shined. He carried a swagger stick beneath his arm. "Fall in!" he bellowed suddenly.

Now it begins, Zack thought.

"I said fall in, you slimy worms!" the sergeant howled. "Heels on that white line! Come on. Do it! Attin-hut!"

Zack's heels were on the line before anyone's.

He glanced quickly to his right and left as the others stumbled into position, then he stared straight ahead. He noticed that the sergeant's name was Foley.

As the candidates assembled, Foley shook his head in disbelief. "What a raggedy-assed group they sent me this time." He turned to the side and spat on the concrete. "Now, when I say 'understand,' I want all of you turkeys and turkettes to say 'yes, sir.' Understand?"

"Yes, sir!" The group's response was uneven.

"Louder!" Foley bellowed.

"Yes, sir!"

Foley whirled and stared at the administration building for a moment, then turned back to his new charges. "I don't believe what I'm seeing! Where've you people been all your lives, at an orgy?"

Zack had to fight back a smile at that one.

"You been doin' too much of that listening to Mick Jagger and bad-mouthing your country." Foley strode down the ranks, drinking in the new faces in front of him, squinting at them as though in search of some fatal weakness. He stopped in front of another black man. "What's your name?"

"Perryman, sir!"

"Well, stop eyeballin' me, Perryman. You are not worthy enough to look your superiors in the eye. Use your peripheral vision. Do you understand me?"

"Yes, sir!" Perryman bellowed.

Foley strode back to the center of the group. He suddenly seemed to become more human, and his lips curled into a little smile. "Hey, folks, we ain't stupid around here. We know why you all come. But before you get to sell what we teach you over at United Airlines, you gotta give the Navy six years of your life, Sweet Pea. Lotta things can happen in six years. We could even get into another war in six years. And if any of you are too peaceful to dump napalm on an enemy village where there might be women and children, I'm gonna find that out. Understand?"

"Yes, sir!" the group yelled.

Foley paced in front of them, stopping this time in front of the big guy next to Zack and giving him a smile. "Hi, son."

"How ya doin', Sarge?"

Foley's eyes became instantly crazed. "What'd you call me?"

The candidate began to tremble. "Pardon?"

"What's your name, boy?"

"Worley, sir. Sid Worley."

"What'd you call me, Worley?"

"I called you 'Sarge.'"

"Before that?"

"I didn't call you anything before that."

Foley put his face a few inches from Worley's. "You said, 'How're *you*.' I am not a ewe, boy! A ewe is a female sheep, boy! Is that what you think I am, boy?"

"No," Worley said.

"No, what!" Foley screamed.

"No, sir!"

"Louder, Sweet Pea!"

"No, sir!" Worley bellowed.

"Do you want to fuck me up the ass, boy! Is that why you called me a ewe? Are you a queer, Worley?"

"No, sir."

Foley stared at him for a moment. "Where you from, boy?"

"Oklahoma, sir."

"Oklahoma?"

"Oklahoma City, sir."

Foley shook his head. "Only two things I know come out of Oklahoma, boy. Steers and queers. Which one are you, boy?"

Worley said nothing.

"I don't see any horns on you, so you must be queer."

"No, sir," Worley muttered.

Foley gave him a big grin. "Stop whispering, Sweet Pea, you're giving me a hard on."

Zack couldn't contain a little chuckle, knowing beforehand that Foley wouldn't let it go.

"You laughing at me, dick-brain?" the sergeant asked.

"No, sir!" Zack yelled.

Suddenly Foley's face was right up in his, but Zack stared right past him, feeling unintimidated.

"You'd better stop eyeballing me, boy, or I'll rip out your eyes and skull-fuck you to death."

Zack kept a straight face and said nothing.

"What's your name?"

"Zack Mayo, sir!"

Foley looked him over and snorted. "How did you slip into this program, Mayo? I didn't know the Navy was so hard up." He pointed to the

Band-Aid on Zack's arm. "You got an injury there, Mayo?"

"Not exactly, sir," Zack said.

"I'll bet." Foley reached out and tore off the Band-Aid, smiled at Zack, then leaned over and inspected the eagle tattoo. "Where'd you get this, Mayo? This is really wonderful work."

Zack fought his embarrassment and responded coolly. "Subic Bay, sir. In the Philippines."

Foley nodded. "I thought I recognized the work." He stared into Zack's eyes again. "Be proud of those wings. They're the only ones you're gonna leave here with, Mayo-naise." He gave Zack a knowing nod, then moved on to his next victim.

Zack stared out at the admin building, more sorry that he'd covered the tattoo than that everyone knew about it. Still, he'd handled himself pretty well.

"You a college boy, Della Serra?" Foley said to the young man further down the line.

"Yes, sir!" Della Serra crowed proudly. "I graduated with honors from Texas Tech, sir. Math major, sir!"

"You don't say." Foley held up his swagger stick and pointed to it. "See this cane, Della Serra? See these little notches near the handle? There's a notch for every college puke like you, Della Serra, who I got to D.O.R.—that's Drop On Request—from this program. And the first one I want to carve out of this class is you, Emiliano." He gave Della Serra an evil look and turned away.

Again Foley paced in front of the candidates, pounding the swagger stick into the palm of his left hand. "I expect to lose half of you before I'm finished. And I will use every means at my disposal, fair or unfair, to get rid of you cockroaches. You got to remember that I love watching you hot shits fail, and I'm always gonna be there, lookin' to trip you up, looking to expose your weaknesses as potential aviators and as human beings. The price at the other end is a flight education worth one million dollars, but first you have to get past me." He gave them his most sadistic smile, then suddenly snapped to attention. "Open your suitcases for inspection."

The candidates dropped to their knees and quickly began arranging their packs and suitcases on the pavement. As Foley walked past the girl Zack had noticed, he lowered his swagger stick and speared a pair of lacy underwear from her belongings. "What's your name, candidate?"

"Casey Seeger, sir!" The girl sounded off as though she had a pair of balls.

Foley held the underpants aloft like a little flag. "Seeger, are we going to have to watch you run around in these for the next thirteen weeks?"

She reached for the undies, but Foley held them higher, shaking them a little bit.

"Some girls will do almost anything to get laid, Seeger. Are you one of those girls? Did you put in for A.O.C.S. to get gang-banged, Seeger?"

Seeger gave Foley a hostile look, her face

turning red. "Sir, you can yell at me if that's what you're supposed to do. But you have no right to insult me, sir!"

"No right?" Foley's face hardened, and he pushed it to within inches of Seeger's. "I'll call you a beaver sandwich if I want to. I'll call you anything I damn well please until the day they commission you an officer and a gentleman and I have to call you 'sir.'" He stared at her for a moment longer, then held up the swagger stick and pointed to the notches. "If my language offends you, Seeger, maybe you ought to D.O.R. If my language offends you, maybe the Navy's not for you, 'cause you're gonna hear ten times worse out in the fleet." He shook her undies loose from the stick, gave her a sneer, then walked to the center of the group. "Okay, you've got five seconds to put your suitcases in order and prepare to move out." He took a breath. "Time's up. Attin-hut! Left-humph! Fo-wud-harch!"

Zack noticed that besides himself, Seeger and Worley were the only ones able to keep up with Foley's commands.

They let the women keep a little hair. Zack reckoned that was all right, although if you wanted to get real gung ho on this equality stuff, maybe the women ought to have been shaved bald as a baby's butt—like himself. Della Serra, whose hair had been the longest, was the last one out of the barber shop, and as he came down the stairs, Foley stopped him and turned him toward his fellow candidates. "Now, this is my idea of an ass-bandit," Foley said. "Wait'll some of our local girls get a look at you, scrotum-head."

The class burst into guffaws, and it seemed as if Sid Worley would be unable to contain himself. He stopped laughing when Foley moved toward him.

"You think that's funny, Worley? Well, let me tell you all something, something you better listen to. I'm not the only obstacle that can trip you up around here. Some of 'em aren't even on this base." He strolled along in front of the candidates, a wise smile on his face. "As long as there's been a Navy base here, there's been what you might as well call your Puget Sound debs, poor girls who come across the sound on the ferry every weekend for one reason." He pointed his swagger stick at the men. "To marry themselves a naval aviator."

The candidates gave him a skeptical look. A couple of them even groaned. Zack stared at Foley, taking in every word.

Foley held out his hand to silence them. "Now a Puget deb will tell you, 'Honey, don't y'all worry 'bout no contraceptives. I got that all taken care of.'" Foley shook his head. "Well, don't you believe a word of it, Sweet Pea, 'cause a Puget deb will do anything and say anything to trap you." He paused a moment to let his words sink in. "And once she's got you by the balls, child, you're probably gonna find yourself with a couple of income tax deductions you didn't have when you came here."

A few of the candidates laughed.

"Go ahead on," Foley said. "I know it sounds silly, especially in this so-called modern age. You scuzzy college pukes may think you're smart, but you're gonna need more than smarts to deal with the debs. They're out there, believe me. And you, Sweet Pea, are the answer to their dreams." Again Foley paused, then suddenly snapped to attention. "Now line up in formation! It's time to get you poopies dressed."

The debs, Zack thought, as he went along the line in the supply room, drawing his uniforms. The goddamn debs. The word came back to him like the taste of some food that he wished to forget. His mother and her friends were always going on about the debs in Norfolk. Maybe his mother had even been one. How the hell else did she end up with Byron? Zack guessed there must be Pensacola debs and Corpus Christi debs and San Diego debs and debs everywhere the Navy docked. Just like the bars and flophouses and pawnshops. Part of the territory. Well, no deb was going to tie this man down.

Seeger and Worley were ahead of him, and Foley met them on the stairs as they came out carrying their uniforms. He gave them all a big grin. "How do you like my poopie factory, Seeger? You enter these doors an individual with a look that's all yours, a style, a way about you, even a personality. And then you come out a poopie." Foley leaned back and guffawed. "Sort of like what happens to food. It goes in looking all fancy and pretty, then..."

"I got the picture, sir!" Seeger bellowed.

"Hey, you're a smart one, Seeger," Foley said.

Worley nudged Zack and nodded at a recruiting poster on the wall. "I knew those commercials were full of shit," he said.

Foley lined up the candidates and double-timed them over to the indoctrination barracks. He left them running in place as he opened the doors. "This is it, children. This is where you live. This is Poopieville. Now double-time your sorry asses up those stairs and find your rooms. Girl poopies to the left, boy poopies to the right."

Zack sprinted up the stairs with his gear and quickly found a door with the names Daniels, Mayo, Perryman, and Worley on it. He tossed his gear on the upper bunk by the window, then jumped up on the bed just as his roommates entered. Perryman, the black man, gave Zack a look. "How do you figure that's your bunk?"

Zack shrugged. "He said it's up to us, and I got here first, didn't I?"

Worley tossed his stuff on the other top bunk. "Whatever you say, Mayo-naise."

Zack jumped down, then all four men began to put their gear into their lockers. Foley's voice boomed from the hallway, "Fall out on the lawn in five minutes. In your poopie suits!"

Topper Daniels, the youngest looking of the four, watched Perryman tape a photo of a woman and two young children in his locker. "You're a married man, huh, Perryman?"

Perryman eyed him for a moment, then nodded. "They're the main reason I'm here."

Daniels shook his head and pulled on his baggy pants. "I still can't believe I did this. I've got a three-point-eight average from Amherst College, and I signed up to be jerked around by this Foley moron."

Perryman laughed. "He just playin' the game, man. Same as everybody else."

Zack stowed his locker like an expert and was surprised to find Worley doing the same to his. He gave him a questioning look.

Worley flashed him a big Okie grin. "I'm a service brat, pal. Same as you."

Zack grinned back and nodded. Then he pulled five new packs of playing cards out of a pair of pants and hid them beneath his skivvies.

Worley shook his head. "Someday you'll have to tell me about Subic."

"Someday." Both men began getting into their poopie suits.

"That Foley looks like he's been through a war or two," Worley said.

Zack shrugged. "I've seen better."

And again the D.I.'s voice boomed from the hallway. "Fall out, worms! Fall out!"

The thirty-six candidates lined up outside, looking remarkably similar—even the women— in their poopie outfits and chrome helmet liners. Zack lined up next to Seeger and in front of Sid Worley. Foley was nowhere to be seen.

"Hey," Sid said, "you think there's any truth to what he was saying about those girls?"

Zack nodded.

"You think that shit's still going on?"

"Sure it is, Sweet Pea," Zack said. "But I also think he should've warned these scuzzy female types about the Puget dudes." He used his peripheral vision to catch a grin on Seeger's face. "Yeah, they'll tell you they're wearing a rubber, but they've bit a little hole in the end."

"You're pretty funny, Mayo," Seeger said.

"Seeger, Mayo, and Worley!" Foley screamed from behind them. "Get on your faces and do push-ups until *I* get tired."

The trio hesitated for a moment.

"Move!" Foley howled.

They stepped out of the formation, got down, and started pushing. Zack tried to make it look as if the push-ups were hard, but he knew he could do at least a hundred. Seeger was starting to fade after ten.

"Havin' trouble, See-gar?"

"No, sir," she wheezed.

All Zack could see were the shiny tops of Foley's shoes. He used his peripheral vision once again to watch Seeger crumple to the ground after sixteen.

Foley let out a soft laugh. "Well, Sugar Britches, it looks like you need a little work on your upper body strength."

Casey Seeger said nothing.

"Is that right, See-gar?"

"Yes, sir," she gasped.

"You'll never make it, weak as you are. Now get up and get back in that formation."

Worley stopped and started to stand up.

"Not you, worm!" Foley said. "You neither, Mayo-naise. You two do push-ups forever!"

"Thirty-nine, forty," Zack muttered.

3

There had been times during her three years at the National Paper Mill that Paula Pokrifki thought she might go insane if she saw another brown bag. She once dreamed of them pouring off the conveyor belt and suffocating her, and in another grotesque nightmare they flew out of her mouth like bats when she tried to speak. Think positively, she told herself; be tough. She knew it was almost quitting time, but she had resolved not to look at her watch or the large clock on the wall until the whistle blew. The time went faster when you didn't see it. Another bundle of bags slid down the shiny metal chute, and Paula neatened the edges, wound string around the stack, and shoved it onto the conveyor belt to her right. She eyed Daisy Mills at the other end of the conveyor; Daisy was fifty-five and seldom missed a day of work. How the hell did she do it? Paula had recently seen a man on the news who was retiring after twenty-seven years of stepping on and off bathroom scales to assure their accuracy. Maybe the older people were right; you *could* get used to anything. But she was damned if she was going to.

The whistle sounded, and the conveyor belt came to a halt. Paula stepped back and exhaled, then pulled the plugs out of her ears. She looked over at her friend Lynette Pomeroy, whose face had suddenly come alive with anticipation of the evening's activities. "Come on, Paula," Lynette yelled. "It's five o'clock."

"Could've fooled me," Paula said.

"Well, let's go then."

Paula nodded and followed her friend to the exit. She felt like a cow being turned out to pasture.

"What's the matter?" Lynette asked as they left the factory.

Paula shook her head. "Just sad to be leaving this beautiful place, is all."

"You're real funny."

"And oh, so happy in my work," Paula said. She waved to her mother, who was getting into an old Toyota with Helen Smith. "'Bye, Mom. See you later."

Esther Pokrifki waved sadly and got into the car.

Paula shoved Lynette. "C'mon, before she decides to ask me what time I'm coming home." Paula turned her back on her mother and almost ran for Lynette's battered Falcon.

When they got to the car, Lynette gave her

a look. "Jesus, Paula, you're twenty-one now. You don't have to answer to her for everything."

"I don't have to, and I don't want to. Let's go."

"Okay, okay. I want to get over there just as bad as you do." Lynette fired up the car and drove out of the parking lot. "Who do you suppose'll be there tonight?"

"The names'll all be the same. It's only the faces that change."

Lynette looked at her. "What's that supposed to mean?"

"I don't know." Paula stared out at the gray waters of the sound. "Maybe it's the other way around."

"Hey, c'mon," Lynette said. "Get changed."

"Roger." Paula reached into the backseat for her makeup kit and positioned it on her lap. She flipped down the visor, adjusted the mirror, pulled off her scarf, and took out her pin curls. She combed out her hair and tried to work on her positive attitude. She was no longer thrilled with going over to the base and being eyeballed by the horny trainees, maybe getting a date with an officer or a flight candidate looking to get laid. That was the negative side. But at least going over there was better than hanging around the local bars or watching T.V. at home under her father's suspicious eye. Besides, every once in a while she did meet some interesting person with a decent education from a different part of the country, someone she could learn something from.

Her hair finished, she slid down in the seat,

took off her blouse, and pulled her emerald green disco dress over her head. Then she took off her jeans, folded them, and put them in the back-seat.

"Hey, you look great," Lynette said.

Paula smiled at her friend. "You never get tired of it, do you, Lynette?"

Lynette pointed her thumb back toward the paper mill and in the direction of their homes. "That's what I'm tired of. And that's what I'm getting out of."

Paula nodded. She was going to get out herself, but she'd given up counting on some Navy man to marry her and take her away. In a year she'd have enough money saved, and then she could either go traveling for a while or move to some other place and start going to school. Junior college, she guessed. Her grades weren't exactly going to get her into Harvard. If she had an education she could pretty much choose her own life. Maybe she'd even enroll in the flight training program as some girls were doing now.

On the ferry the girls changed seats, and Lynette made herself up and changed her clothes, flipping the bird to some guy in a black Cheyenne pickup who was giving her the eye. Lynette looked so serious whenever they got ready to go over to the base. You'd think she would have learned by now. Guys didn't come to Port Rainier looking for wives. And even if they did, girls like Paula and Lynette weren't the kind they were after. Don't think about it, Paula, she told herself. Just enjoy yourself. Just have the best time you can. "Lookin' good," she said. Lynette's blond hair was perfectly combed, and her huge breasts hung halfway out of her purple dress. Paula was more petite, but petite girls' figures lasted longer.

Everything on the base always looked neat. The old wooden buildings gleamed with white paint and green trim, the grass was full and perfectly cut, and even the streets and sidewalks looked as if they had been washed down. They probably had—by some poor enlisted man. Well, that was the way of the world, Paula thought. No sense worrying about it. "There's Nellie now." Paula pointed to the steps of one of the buildings where a woman in her fifties, the base social director, was speaking with a young officer.

Lynette parked the car and grabbed a stack of record albums off the backseat. The girls walked up the sidewalk, waving at the woman on the steps. "Hi, Mrs. Rufferwell," Lynette said.

"Well, hello, Lynette and Paula." She gestured to the young lieutenant at her side. "Allow me to introduce Ensign Burns. Timothy Burns from Milwaukee, Wisconsin. This is Paula Pokrifki and Lynette Pomeroy."

"Nice to meet you," he said, eyeing Lynette's cleavage.

They both said hello.

"Well, thanks, Mrs. Rufferwell," he said, shaking the lady's hand. He nodded to Paula and Lynette. "Hope to see you gals again."

"Feeling's mutual," Lynette said. Paula just smiled.

After he had gone, Mrs. Rufferwell said, "Such a pleasant young man."

Lynette handed her the record albums.

"Thank you, thank you," Nellie Rufferwell said. "But I do hope you girls didn't come all the way over here just to bring me these records."

"No, ma'am," Lynette said. "We planned on stopping at the O. Club tonight, one way or the other."

Nellie gave them an approving smile.

"Be seeing you," Paula said.

"'Bye, girls, and thanks again," Nellie said. "By the way, the Blue Angels'll be in next month. If you'd like me to fix you up, just let me know."

"That'd be fantastic!" Lynette said.

The girls turned and started down the stairs.

As Zack counted his sixtieth push-up, Sid said, "Oh, my god!"

Zack looked over at him, wondering if the Okie was about to be sick. "What?"

Sid continued to do push-ups, but he was looking across the street, not at the ground. "Would you look at that," he said.

Zack raised his head and watched two girls descend the stairs.

"I mean," Sid said, "that's one bodacious pair of ta-tas on that blonde."

Zack grunted and did more push-ups. He never was partial to blondes. He thought the other girl was cuter, but he also thought that girls were something he shouldn't be thinking about right now.

"You blind?" Sid said.

Zack was about to say something when Foley bellowed, "Faster, Worley. You ain't got no time to be runnin' your mouth in this place without my authorization. Run it again and you'll be doin' push-ups till sunrise!"

"Seventy-four," Zack muttered. "Seventy-five."

"Far fucking out!" Lynette said before they were even fifty feet away from Nellie Rufferwell.

"Watch your mouth, Lynette," Paula said. "Someone might overhear." Not that Nellie Rufferwell hadn't heard it all. A high-class madam was about all she was.

Lynette covered her mouth and snickered. "I've been wanting to meet one of the Blue Angels since I can remember. Old Nellie's lookin' out for us."

"Thank God for good old Nellie." Paula stopped for a moment to watch the two officer candidates doing push-ups across the street.

"Look at the new poopies," Lynette said.

"Poor guys." The girls started to walk.

Lynette waved at them. "See you guys in a month when you get liberty."

Paula rubbed her head and smiled. "Don't worry. It grows out about an inch by then." She turned away when she caught the scowl of the tall, black, drill instructor. Those guys must be a barrel of laughs, she thought. She looked back again at the women in the formation. A few lucky breaks and she could have been one of them. Maybe in her next incarnation.

On the steps of the officers club they met Donny Tarlton, a handsome flight instructor from Houston. He had just finished a brief affair with one of Paula's friends from the paper mill, and he had been so cruel when he dumped her that the girl hadn't been able to work for a week.

"Hi, Donny," Lynette said.

"How you girls doin'? Haven't seen you around for a while, Paula. When we goin' out?"

"Word's out about you, Donny," she said.

His eyes suddenly got cold. "That right?"

Lynette grabbed Paula's arm. "Paula!"

"Charlotte Moss says hello," Paula said.

Donny shook his head. "I reckon you debs do talk, don't you?"

"It's free." Paula sneered at Donny and pushed through the door.

"You didn't have to do that," Lynette said when they were inside.

"Yeah, I know."

"Well?"

"Well, what?" Paula said. "I don't like people who dump on my friends."

Lynette looked at the floor. "Come on, Paula. Let's just have a good time."

Paula stared at Lynette for a moment, then gave her a smile. "Why not," she said. "Let's get a drink."

The two girls walked toward the bar, Lynette inspecting every man in sight.

4

Although the sunlight filtering through the trees that overhung the narrow trail was beautiful, Zack found that by keeping his eyes on Casey Seeger's buttocks bouncing along in front of him as he ran, his attitude was much better and his stamina seemed to increase. He was always happy to discover a new trick of survival.

"Flyin' low and feelin' mean!" Foley bellowed in a singsong voice.

The candidates repeated his line, Zack wondering how the hell Foley managed to do it. How could he get up for this bullshit every day, run like hell, and barely break a sweat?

"Spot a family by a stream."

"Spot a family by a stream," the candidates repeated.

"Pickle a pair and hear 'em scream."

"Pickle a pair and hear 'em scream."

"'Cause napalm sticks to kids." Foley let go with a little chuckle as he finished the line.

Hardass Foley, Zack thought, as he hollered out the line. Getting his troops ready to be hardass bombers. The thought of actually dropping bombs on people was seldom in Zack's mind, even though he had met plenty of fliers in the Philippines who had dropped more explosives on Vietnam than they could remember. Zack wasn't in it for that, although he supposed he would do it as well as anyone if he had to. He just wanted to go a thousand miles an hour into the wild blue yonder.

"Eighteen kids in a free fire zone."

"Eighteen kids in a free fire zone."

"Books under arms, just walkin' on home."

Zack repeated, then took in a deep breath of the fresh salt air.

"La-ast kid walks home alone."

Zack bellowed it out, then took his eyes off Casey's behind to look at the blue gray ocean as the candidates burst out on the beach.

"'Cause napalm sticks to kids."

"'Cause napalm sticks to kids." And this goddamn sand is goddamn hard to run in with these goddamn boondocker boots. They turned at the water's edge where the sand was a little harder and headed for the tunnel that led to the gun emplacements. Fun, fun, fun, Zack thought, locking his eyeballs on Seeger's ass once again. Nice hunks of muscle.

Sid Worley ran ahead of Casey, and as he splashed up some water he turned and looked at her, displaying his big Okie grin. "Hey, Seeger, what're you doing in this program?"

"Same as you," she gasped.

"Same as me?" Sid wheezed.

"What's the matter, Worley?" she asked. "Am I threatening you?"

"Not this hoss," he replied.

"Hey, Casey," Zack said.

She flashed a look over her shoulder. "What, Mayo?"

"You could get sent to war, you know?"

"That's part of the program."

"You could get your cute little ass shot down."

"Don't lose any sleep over it, Mayo."

"Oh, I won't," he said.

She took a deep breath. "Besides, I wouldn't mind being the first woman to fly a jet fighter in combat."

"Great," Zack said. "You can go in my place." She wouldn't last too long in a POW camp.

Sid looked over his shoulder again. "Are you really going for jets, Casey?"

She nodded. "All the way."

"How about you, Mayo?" he said a little louder.

"Jets," Zack said.

"I hate to tell you guys," Sid said, "but they only take two out of every class for jets. Which one of you is going with me?"

Before either Zack or Casey could reply, Foley's voice boomed out again. "Okay, worms, here's my favorite. And I want you to sound off like it's your favorite too. Understand?"

"Yes, sir!" the candidates yelled.

Foley sang, and the future aviators echoed his lines. "Family of gooks sittin' in a ditch. Baby suckin' on her mama's tit. Dow Chemical don't give a shit. That napalm sticks to kids." Foley let out an absolutely evil laugh as his troops disappeared into the tunnel.

"Guy's got a real sense of humor, doesn't he?" Worley said.

Zack couldn't even see Casey's butt in the darkness. A dim circle of light was visible about a hundred feet in front of them, and because Zack knew what awaited them on the other side of the tunnel, he decided to keep his mouth shut and listen to the rhythmic clomp of the boots and the accentuated gasping for breath. He felt as if he were inside an iron lung.

He could hear the noncoms shouting before he emerged into the hazy sunlight. Don't take it personally, he reminded himself. The gun emplacement bunker had been built in 1895, and the massive, three-story chunk of concrete now served as an outside torture chamber for the aviation officer candidates. At each landing of the time-weathered staircases stood a D.I., pounding his swagger stick against his palm and hurling insults at the fatigued and terrified troops. A mammoth white sergeant locked his piggy little eyes on Zack and raised his swagger stick as though he were going to beat him. "Move out, slime bag!" he yelled, then pointed at Seeger. "And if that beaver in front of you passes out, you run right over her." Zack said nothing, suppressing an urge to laugh. He wasn't hurting nearly as bad as many of his classmates. He wondered if the ambulance and the two medics off to the side were there for expected casualties or merely for psychological intimidation.

"Do you love this training, lady?" one of the D.I.'s bellowed at Seeger.

"Yes, sir!" she gasped, turning and mounting another set of stairs.

"Then you're crazy," the D.I. shouted at her back.

Zack gave him a look.

"Run, come-bubble!" the D.I. said. "I'm too pretty for you to be lookin' at."

All except for your face, Zack thought. He ran on, planting his feet methodically on every concrete step, being careful not to slip. He gave Casey's buttocks only an occasional glance. He was glad to be behind her because she wasn't that fast, although she was better than half the guys. She'd probably done a lot of running in college. Doubtless a ball-buster too.

Coleman went down first, passing out after descending the stairs and anticipating the start of a second climb. The medics bent over him for a moment, then pulled him off to the side where he lay gasping beneath a tree. Trent, a woman, keeled over after getting to the top of the gun emplacement for the third time, and two D.I.'s laid her on the cool concrete while tears ran down her face. Zack didn't feel much as he ran past her. That was what the program was for: to weed out people who couldn't take it. Everyone knew that the whole class wouldn't graduate. His own lungs felt as if they were on fire, and his heart was thumping so hard he thought it might jump out of his chest, but he was still a long way from the outer edge of his endurance. There was a kind of white heat in his legs, and he could barely feel them, but his brain kept moving one in front of the other. The strain drove everything else out of your mind, and there was something about that that Zack liked. Must be like what an animal feels. He glanced at the faces of a couple of his classmates, faces from which the veneer of civilization had vanished and on which only the hunger for survival remained.

Zack finished the course for the third time and crossed the finish line, stealing a quick look at Foley. The D.I. was shaking his head, and nothing showed on his face but contempt. Tough titty if he doesn't like it, Zack thought. Then he dropped to his knees next to Sid and Casey, and he closed his eyes and sucked in the cool air. When he finally looked around, everyone else had finished. Perryman lay on his back, holding his stomach; Della Serra knelt beside a tree, barfing up his breakfast.

"That's it, Emiliano!" Foley yelled. "That's the kind of talk I like to hear from you tough guys."

Della Serra tried to nod, but his body shook suddenly from another retch.

Foley sneered. "I'll take your D.O.R. anytime, Mr. Math Major from Texas Tech." He pointed off to the side. "Eyes, right!"

His exhausted troops looked over to see an

advanced class of about twenty candidates double-timing toward them, smiles on their faces as they sang cadence. They were dressed in bright blue warm-up suits with the words *Thraxton's Cobras* emblazoned across the front. "Would you look at that," Worley said.

Zack nodded, his head turning slowly as the troops ran by. They looked happy and fresh, and they'd probably already run a couple of miles. They all had nicknames on the backs of their sweatshirts—*Hoosier Face, The Barber, Animal House, Chow Hog, Baby Huey, The Professor*—and they ran up and down the steps of the gun emplacement as though they were riding an escalator.

Foley walked among the new candidates as Thraxton's Cobras ate up the course, and after they had gone up and down a couple of times, he turned on his exhausted troops. "That's you in thirteen weeks, poopies. Those of you who make it, that is. You'll notice that their ranks have been thinned out quite a bit. Only the strong survive."

The poopies looked around at one another, but no one looked at anyone for very long.

Foley paced in front of them. "You are without a doubt the most pathetic class that I have ever been assigned. That's quite a first, because I've seen some mighty sorry bags of crap in my time." He stared at them for a moment, then shrugged. "However, I have been instructed by the commanding officer to inform you that if, by some miracle, you should get secured by four weeks from today, you will be allowed to go to the regimental ball where you may mingle with local talent of the opposite gender."

More groans of relief escaped the poopies, and several of them broke into big smiles.

Sid nudged Zack. "All right," he said, his enthusiasm quickly rekindled.

"Don't think it's gonna be that easy," Foley said. He popped his palm with his swagger stick. "No human being has ever found four weeks with me easy." He paraded back and forth in front of them, his white teeth glistening in his best smile.

Foley was right—it wasn't easy, and it wasn't going to get easy, and the only person who would find it easy would have to be a masochist with a great deal of stamina. Zack was no masochist, but over the first few days he didn't find a lot to complain about. He always enjoyed the physical exercise, and he could handle the mental torture because he knew who he was, and he knew exactly why he was here. He'd been around the military long enough to know what the treatment was all about, and there was no way he was going to let it cause him to lose his focus.

He also enjoyed studying his classmates and trying to figure out which ones would drop. He could already see it starting in a few of them— the sad look in the eyes, the lack of concentration during exercise, the constant irritation with the rapid changes that Foley was always throwing at them. Zack found it best to make his mind a blank, to never expect anything to go on for very long, mainly to never get too comfortable. If you got too comfortable, then you started getting irritated when things changed, and that was when Foley would zero in like a wasp and sting your ass right out of the program. Zack guessed it helped not to have any outside concerns. His roommate Perryman had a family, a family he worried about, and one day in the chow line, when he fucked up while they were counting off, Foley asked him if he didn't want to quit right then and join his wife and kids. Perryman was the only black man in the program, and Zack guessed that Foley would ride him pretty hard. He'd try to make him feel insecure about commanding white men, especially rednecks who'd just as soon shoot him as look at him. That would be Perryman's problem, and Zack knew that you didn't get very far worrying about other people's problems. Foley would probably find one of Zack's before too long.

Zack had always been a fast eater, so the couple of minutes they got to gobble their chow didn't bother him that much. He was almost always hungry, and even the shit-on-shingle that they ate so much of tasted good. Foley tortured them at meals by making them wait. They had to stand at attention while the smell of the food filled their nostrils, then sit down simultaneously at Foley's command. If anyone was too fast or too slow, the entire group stood up again, and they'd keep repeating the exercise until they got it right. From this Zack learned not to anticipate, to stay with whatever they were doing until it was finished, then move on to the next thing. If you started looking forward to things too much you'd surely fuck up, then you'd get frustrated, and then you'd make some fatal mistake. Roll with the punches, bend with the breeze, don't resist unless you know that's what they want. You didn't really have to give up your personality; you just didn't have to bother showing it.

However, it was nice to see a little hair growing back in after a couple of weeks. A reminder that your personality was still there, beneath the surface. As Zack looked at himself in the bathroom mirror and gently patted the half-inch of stubble, Della Serra stood beside him, running an electric shaver over his dome. "You should stop worrying about it, Mayo," Della Serra said. "Just do like me."

"You're gonna be pretty all your life, Emiliano." Zack snapped him with his towel and stepped out of the latrine. Della Serra had boundless enthusiasm, and Zack figured he'd make it through the program. That math background didn't hurt him in aerodynamics either. If Zack had any weak spot, that's where it was. He started toward his room, then turned and ducked past the stairwell and opened the door to Seeger's room.

"Morning, ladies." He just stood there grinning at them.

Gonzales leaped up from her bed and quickly slid on a uniform. Casey had on her fatigue pants and a bra, and she simply shook her head at Zack before going back to spit shining her boondockers. "Ever heard of knocking, Mayo?" she asked.

"A while back," he said.

"What do you want?" Gonzales asked, buttoning up her fatigue shirt.

"You guys hear about Sands and Kantrowitz?"

"What?" Casey asked.

"They D.O.R.'d. Last night."

Casey stopped her polishing and looked at him. "That's too bad."

He nodded. "Breaks my heart."

"First I've heard of your having one."

"C'mon, See-gar. This is a game of survival— survival of the fittest."

"No need to be so happy about it."

"Hey, it's less competition."

Casey shook her head. "The whole world's a jungle, huh, Zack?"

"That's pretty close."

"Dog eat dog, down to the last one, right?"

"You got it, Sweet Pea." He looked at her breasts. "Good shine on those boonies, Seeger."

"You ready for inspection?"

"I stay ready." He gave her a little grin and headed back toward his room.

His roommates were rushing around in a frenzy, preparing for Foley's eagle-eye inspection. Worley was lining up his shoes and boots under the bunk, Perryman was Brassoing his belt buckle, and Topper Daniels, who seemed in a genuine panic, was folding his underwear, measuring them with a ruler, and putting them in his locker. He seemed very relieved to see

Zack. "Where you been, Mayo? Inspection's in five minutes. Give 'em to me."

Zack held out his hand. "Where's your money?"

Topper handed him five dollars. "There. Now come on."

Zack jumped up on his bunk and pried a piece of fiberboard loose from the ceiling.

Perryman gave him a contemptuous look. "You'd better hope Foley never finds out about that, Mayo."

"Foley don't know everything." Zack reached up in the ceiling and pulled out a pair of perfectly spit-shined boots. He handed them down to Topper, then grabbed a belt buckle and held it up for Perryman to see. "Two bucks a buckle, Perryman. Look at that shine. Boonies'll cost you five."

"Shee-it!" Perryman said. "Who's got two bucks? It costs me every penny of my pay just to keep my old lady and kids in that motel."

Zack shrugged.

"Hey, man," Sid said. "You got some enlisted guy doing that for you?"

"These are deep dark secrets of the trade." Zack put the buckle away and replaced the fiberboard. He jumped down from the bed.

"You're really something, Mayo," Perryman said.

"That's what she said," Zack replied.

"Just tell me this. Is the piss-ass money you're making off this worth the risk of getting us all kicked out of here on an honor violation?"

"Honor violation?"

"Yeah. You ever heard of that?"

Zack gave Perryman a little grin. "I don't notice anyone complaining," he said.

"Aw..." Perryman turned away and put his can of Brasso back in his locker.

Zack shrugged at Worley, then checked his own belt buckle to make sure it was ready for inspection.

Zack passed Della Serra doing the low crawl, then scrambled to his feet and raced toward the horizontal ladder. The obstacle course was his favorite part of the training, probably because it was the thing he was best at. It took his mind off aerodynamics. He could run the course faster than anyone, and even Foley had told him that if he could keep improving he would easily break the course record before his training was completed—that is, if he didn't wash out because he couldn't understand the mumbo jumbo in aerodynamics. He'd have to figure a way around that.

Perryman was a quarter of the way through when Zack jumped on the horizontal ladder, and when Zack dropped off, Perryman was still struggling to finish.

"Lookin' good, Mayo-naise!" Foley shouted. "Now get your ass over the wall." His classmates shouted encouragement from the finish line.

Zack grabbed the rope and walked up the ten-foot wooden wall as though he were Spider Man, pivoted at the top, and dropped to the ground below. He took a deep breath and sprinted the last fifty yards to the finish line where a few cheering candidates slapped him on the back. He ran past them, finally stopping by an old backstop thirty yards from the end of the obstacle course. He leaned against the wood, sucking air, watching the trainees cheer each other on. He had to get that course record; maybe it would make up for his poor performance in aerodynamics.

He sat down and stared at the ground for a moment. When he looked up, his classmates were still yelling to the stragglers, but Foley was staring straight at him. What the hell was the matter now? Their eyes locked for a moment, then Foley shook his head and turned away. Zack stood up and moseyed over to the finish line.

Poor Seeger, he thought, watching her struggle halfway up the rope before dropping back to the bottom. Foley watched her too, a slight smile appearing on his lips. Seeger tried again, with no better luck than the first time.

"Seeger!" Foley said.

"Yes, sir," she gasped.

"You ain't gettin' out of here 'til you get over that wall, girl."

She said nothing.

"Seeger!"

"Yes, sir!"

"Did you hear me?"

"Yes, sir."

"What do you have to say for yourself?"

She grabbed the rope and began to pull herself up. "I'll make it, sir."

"Do you want to be a man, See-gar?"

She shook her head, pulling on the rope, barely getting one hand above the other.

"Are you another one of those little girls who never got Daddy's attention, 'cause he really wanted a son?"

She shook her head again.

"Are you one of *those,* See-gar?"

She bit her lip, tried to get her hand up another few inches, then slipped and crumpled back to the ground. She made a valiant effort to hold back her tears, but they suddenly streamed out of her eyes.

"That's it!" Foley yelled. "That's what'll beat you, Seeger, that's what'll beat you every time."

She gave him a questioning look.

He looked away as though he were talking to the wall. "It's your mental attitude as a person of the female persuasion." He stared at her once again. "Under all your bullshit, Seeger, you're still thinking like a second-class citizen. You could never give orders to men."

She looked at the wall, then back at Foley, unable to say anything.

"And you need more strength in your upper body."

"I'll work on it, sir." Her voice was full of determination.

"You do that."

She nodded.

"Now get over there with the rest of the worms."

"Yes, sir." She ran around the wall and joined her classmates at the finish line.

A hardass, Zack thought. A real hardass.

* * *

That night Zack drifted away from the group returning from the P.X., and when he was sure no one had noticed, he headed for the north end of the base. He met Anderson, a taciturn enlisted sailor, next to an old incinerator behind his barracks. "Looks good," Zack said, surveying the boots and belt buckles that Anderson had laid out on a blanket.

"Damn straight," the sailor said, extending his hand.

Zack dropped a couple of bills in the hand. "See you next week."

Anderson nodded. "Sure thing." He stood up and walked away.

Zack folded up the blanket and was about to hoist it over his shoulder when he heard, "So that's how you do it," in the darkness behind him.

"Huh?" His first thought was Foley, but he would have recognized the sergeant's voice.

Sid Worley stepped out of the shadows. "Not a bad scam, Mayo-naise. It's what I figured you were doing."

Zack gave him a guilty look, then shouldered the folded blanket. "Hey, man, you wouldn't tell anyone about this, would you?"

Sid gave him a big grin. "Not me, hoss. That is, if you'd make it worth my while."

"Meaning?"

Sid shrugged. "How about free boonies for the duration?"

Zack stroked his chin as though he were deep in contemplation. "Tell you what," he said.

"You get me through aerodynamics and you can write your own ticket."

Sid slapped him on the back. "Done," he said.

By the time they stood for their one-month inspection, Zack's class had been winnowed to twenty-nine candidates. With Sid's help, Zack had moved from the bottom of the heap to twentieth in aerodynamics, and while that didn't make him Isaac Newton, he could at least survive the program. In everything else he was near the top of his class, and he had no doubt that in another nine weeks Sergeant Foley would be saluting him and calling him *sir*.

He tried not to smile as he watched the sergeant going around their room, looking for dust or improperly made bunks or lockers that weren't up to snuff. But they'd all been over it so many times that nothing could be wrong.

"This shithouse don't look too bad," Foley said, stopping in front of Topper Daniels and eyeballing him from top to bottom. He reached out and pulled a tiny piece of lint off Daniels' shoulder. "Irish pennant, boy."

"Sir?"

"Put yourself on report."

"For what, sir?" Daniels asked.

"Improper uniform." Foley turned to Perryman and pointed at his belt buckle. "Did you shine that buckle, Perryman?"

"Yes, sir."

"With what?"

"Brasso, sir!"

"It looks like you shined it with a Hershey bar."

Perryman began to say something, but Foley turned away. He gave Zack the once-over, then stared at his chin for a moment. "You blinked while you were shaving this morning, Mayonaise."

"Yes, sir," Zack said.

Foley reached out and touched the point of his chin. "You missed a spot."

"It won't happen again, sir."

"You better stop dreamin' about those Puget debs, Mayo. Tend to business."

"Yes, sir."

Foley moved over to Sid and checked him out. "Not bad, Worley."

"Thank you, sir."

"It looks like you've done everything you can."

"Yes, sir."

"Now if your mug wasn't in the hurt locker, you'd be in good shape." Foley looked around quickly, hoping to catch the other candidates smiling, but everyone managed to keep a straight face. "No one even thinks I'm funny anymore."

Foley gave the room another glance, then shook his head. "Marginal, children. Marginal." He paused to let the fear sink in. "But I'm gonna let you all go to the ball. Release some of that tension." He turned and strode out of the room. In the hallway he bellowed, "Class secured! Class secured!"

Sid let go with a rebel yell and threw his hat into the air.

"Women!" Topper yelled. "We're gonna see some real women!"

Perryman slammed the door on his locker. "I gotta go call my wife."

"Get on it, hoss," Sid said. "And lead me to those Puget debs. You ready for it, Mayo?"

"Ready, willing, and able," Zack said. "I'm..." He stopped, looking at Henderson, who had suddenly appeared in the doorway wearing his civvies and carrying the suitcase he had brought to camp. "Hey, Hendy," Zack said.

The others stopped what they were doing and looked at Henderson. He had D.O.R.'d the night before.

"Hey, you guys. I just wanted to say good-bye. Wish you good luck and all that."

"Thanks." Sid walked over and shook his hand.

"Take it easy, man," Perryman said. "Don't let this get you down."

"Naw." Henderson shook his head. "Well, be seeing you." He turned and walked away as the others muttered uncomfortable good-byes.

"Too bad," Sid said.

"I knew he'd never make it," Zack said. "I saw this comin' by the third day."

"Is that right?" Perryman said.

Zack nodded.

"How about me, then?"

"Go call your wife." Zack slapped Perryman on the back. "Tell her I said you'd be chief of staff in twenty years."

Perryman gave him a look.

"See you at the ball tonight," Zack said.

5

Even in his dress white uniform, Zack felt like a goddamn vulture. He and Sid stood off to the side in the officers club, watching the parade of Puget debs—or whoever the hell they were— enter the club in their satiny formals. The girls seemed as nervous as he was as they went through the short receiving line, forcing their hopeful smiles on the officers and their stuffy wives who greeted them. Zack's hunger for a woman had been growing all afternoon, but he hadn't seen anything so far that interested him very much.

He elbowed Sid. "I can't believe it."

"What's that?" Sid kept looking at the arrivals.

"I think I've still got some discrimination left."

"I'm losing mine rapidly," Sid said.

They both watched Topper introduce himself

to a short, chubby, melon-breasted girl and lead her to the dance floor.

"I think the program's gettin' to Topper," Zack said.

"Look at that." Sid pointed to Perryman and his wife, who were locked in a close embrace as they danced to a slow tune. "Married seven years and still in love."

"Something else." Zack shook his head.

"That's what it's all about," Sid said.

Zack elbowed him. "Not tonight it ain't."

"Holy shit!" Sid suddenly grabbed his arm. "It's them."

"Them?" Zack eyed the two women coming through the door. They weren't bad.

"Them! Those two from our first day."

Zack shook his head.

"When we were doing push-ups."

"Oh, yeah." Zack gave Casey the thumbs up as she walked by with a handsome lieutenant J.G.

Sid moaned. "How could you forget that bodacious set of ta-tas?"

"I remember." Zack remembered that they were too big, that he liked the other girl better. Her smaller breasts were pushed up high, a gold cross dangling between them.

"Let's move, partner." Sid led the way over to old Nellie at the end of the receiving line. "Mrs. Rufferwell?"

She turned and gave him a smile. "Yes, Sid."

She probably stayed up nights looking at pictures and memorizing names.

"Ma'am, could you introduce us to these attractive young ladies?"

"My pleasure, boys."

Boys, my ass, Zack thought.

Sid immediately stuck out his hand and grabbed the blonde's.

Nellie smiled at them with maternal approval. "Officer Candidate Sid Worley, may I present Lynette Pomeroy?"

"You may," Sid said. "Pleased to meet you, Lynette."

She gave him a big smile. "Hi."

"Miss Paula Pokrifki," Nellie said, "Sid's classmate Zack Mayo."

Zack nodded.

"Pleased to meet you," Paula said.

Nellie Rufferwell patted the candidates on the back. "Well, I hope you all have a good time."

"Thank you, ma'am," Sid said.

Zack looked at Paula, then glanced nervously at the floor. Christ, he didn't have the slightest idea what to say. He looked at her again and rubbed his head. "You told us it would grow out an inch."

Sid walked behind him and whispered, "It's grown out more than an inch, Sweet Pea."

Zack dropped his eyes and tried not to laugh.

"That was you guys, huh?" Paula asked.

"Screwin' up from day one."

"Well, you're still in the program anyway."

"Oh, yeah," Zack said.

They began walking toward the refreshment

table. "Is this your first night of liberty?" Lynette asked.

"Yes, ma'am," Sid said. "Four long, hard weeks of sacrifice for our country, for our people, and for you all. But we survived."

"Come on." Lynette grabbed his arm. "Let's dance."

Sid gave Zack a look, then turned back to Lynette. "I'm all yours."

Paula and Zack kept walking. "You want to dance?" she asked.

"Let's have some punch. Maybe Nellie put something wild in it."

Paula laughed. "Don't count on it. I think Nellie's gone respectable."

"*Gone's* the word." He poured Paula a cup. "Maybe an extra dose of saltpeter."

"She hasn't gone *that* respectable."

Zack took a sip of punch, looking out at the dance floor where Sid and Lynette were dancing in a tight embrace. He turned back to Paula. "Hey, what kind of name is Pokrifki?"

"Polish."

"Um."

"No jokes?"

"Not a one."

"That's a first." She pulled a loose thread off his uniform. "What kind of name is Mayo?"

"Eye-talian. My mom was Irish, but all I got were her ears. The rest is all wop."

"Where are you from, Mayo the Wop?"

He made a gesture that took in the entire room. "Everywhere and nowhere, Paula the Polack."

"Seriously. Or have you traveled a lot?"

"Sure," he said. "My father's a rear admiral in the seventh fleet."

"Really?" She seemed genuinely excited.

"Really. We've lived áll over the world." He put his finger to his chin and closed his eyes. "Katmandu, Moscow, Nairobi."

"That's really something. I've never been out of Washington except once when I visited this aunt of mine over to Portland." She stopped and shook her head. "Over *at* Portland. Ain't it pathetic the way folks talk around here?" She was actually blushing.

"Your grammar's better than Sergeant Foley's." He squeezed her arm. "Probably better than mine too."

She smiled and watched the dancers for a moment. "Hey, you're puttin' me on."

"Really. My grammar's lousy."

"We ain't got no Navy in Moscow."

"Your geography's better than mine too." He looked her body up and down before finishing his punch.

"Where *are* you from?" she asked.

He shrugged. "A bunch of boring places."

"At least there's a bunch."

"Ain't life grand?" He watched Sid's hand move slowly down Lynette's back.

"You got a girl?" Paula asked.

He looked at her and shook his head. "Ain't lookin' for one either."

"Yeah?" Paula stared brazenly back at him. He liked that.

"Yeah," he said.

"What *are* you lookin' for?"

Zack grinned at her for a moment. "I hear most of the girls who come to these things are looking for husbands."

"Not me."

"They even warned us about you girls."

"It's not my game," she said.

"Why do you come here then?"

"To meet interesting people. To improve myself." She said it as though she really meant it.

"Very commendable."

"You wouldn't believe the losers we got over in Port Angeles."

"Oh, I can imagine." They probably weren't much different than the losers in Norfolk or the Philippines. They probably weren't much different than his father. He could have been there himself without much trouble. "You go to school?"

She shook her head and he watched her pretty brown hair settle on her shoulders. "I work for National Paper."

"Um."

"It's a good job. I make eight twenty-three an hour."

"More than yours truly." He stared at the tops of her breasts.

"When I get enough money saved I'll probably go to college."

"That's good, Paula."

"Where'd you go to school?"

He raised four fingers. "Here and there. I started at a junior college in California and finished in Las Vegas. Made a couple of stops in between."

"At least you finished."

"I did it so I could fly."

She nodded. "I think I'll probably start in junior college."

He stared at the dance floor, saying nothing. He always felt uncomfortable when people got too serious about their dreams.

"Maybe I'll go to California too. Do you think..."

"I think we ought to dance." He put his arm around her, and the touch of the skin on her back was exquisite.

"Oh," she said. "Okay."

He smiled at her tenderly and led her onto the floor.

The music stopped, and Sid and Lynette pulled apart. They stared at each other for a moment as they returned from their passionate imaginings to reality. Sid finally let go with a little laugh. "Wow," he said.

"Yeah." Lynette blinked and looked at the floor, then back at Sid. "Uh, you been through the Dilbert Dunker yet?"

"Naw," he said, glad that she had started some conversation. "But I hear it's a cakewalk."

"That's not what I hear."

Sid shrugged. "Both my dad and my brother went through it. They made it, so I know I can."

"Your brother's a flyer?"

"He was," Sid said. "He died."

"Vietnam?"

Sid nodded.

"I'm sorry. I had a big brother who died over there too." Lynette surveyed the primly dressed officers and candidates. "He wasn't no flyer though. Just your basic Marine Corps type. I was only twelve when it happened, so I don't remember much about him."

"It's too bad," Sid said. "Boy, I sure remember Tommy." He caught Lynette's eye as the music came up. "You mind if we talk about something else?"

Lynette pulled him to her and kissed him on the neck. "We don't have to talk at all."

"That suits me fine." He looked over her shoulder and smiled at Zack.

Zack grinned back at his roommate, happy that Paula had sent a young lieutenant packing when he'd tried to cut in on Zack, and happy to feel her body molding to his as they danced. Across the floor, Topper had his cheek against his partner's chest, and closer by, Della Serra was nibbling the ear of another girl. Were these the wily Puget debs spinning their webs? Who gives a damn, Zack thought.

Paula pulled back so he could see her face. "Think you'll make it all the way to getting your wings?"

"Who knows? I think so, but guys smarter than me have already dropped out."

"Does the program get to you?"

Zack shook his head. "Not so far."

"First few weeks are the worst."

"That's what they say." She probably knew

more about the goddamn program than he did. "But if I've learned anything around here it's that you can't relax. I'm tryin' real hard not to fuck up."

Paula's face grew serious. "Just think to yourself, 'I'm gonna do it.'"

He stepped back and saluted. "Yes, sir!"

"Really." She came back into his arms once again. "You've got to program yourself. You've got to see yourself making it, and then it'll happen."

"You're sure now?"

"I am. I just read this article in *Cosmo* about that very thing."

Zack pulled her close and let out a little laugh.

"You think I'm a joke," she said.

He pulled back to look at her. "I think you're a very pretty girl, Paula."

They looked at each other for a few seconds, then he leaned forward and kissed her gently. He began to pull back, but she put her hand behind his head and slid her tongue into his mouth. Suddenly nothing mattered to him but the exquisite feeling of this woman, and he kissed back strongly and shamelessly, wanting it to go on forever. When Paula finally pushed away from him, they both were gasping as if they had been through the obstacle course.

Her green eyes flashed at him; then she said, "What do you say we flee this pit stop?"

He nodded.

"I'll just get Lynette and Sid."

"Hurry," he said.

* * *

After a long kiss, Zack pulled away and leaned against the seat in the back of Lynette's Falcon. Paula rested her head on his chest. "Lord, have mercy," he said.

Sid turned around and flashed him a grin. "How you doin', good buddy?"

"Never better." Zack managed a weak smile as Paula stroked his leg.

Lynette gave them a quick look. "Think you guys can hold off until we get to the beach?"

"Shut up and drive, Lynette," Paula muttered. Zack was surprised by her seriousness.

"Well excuuuuuse me!" Lynette said.

Sid gave her a kiss, then his head disappeared from Zack's view.

"Cut that out!" Lynette said after a moment. "You want me to crack this thing up?"

"Anything for love," Sid said.

Love, love, love, Zack thought. What the hell was that? He stroked Paula's hair, then bent over and kissed her neck. Don't fool yourself, boy, he said to himself. Four weeks of the treatment'll make a man feel funny things. He had never been in love, but he had never felt for a woman what he was feeling now. "Uh-uh," he muttered.

"Huh?" Paula said.

"Nothing." He rubbed her back and stared out the window at the beacon from a lighthouse that was circling the ocean and beach.

What amazed Sid was Lynette's efficiency. She spread the blanket on the sand, then lay down and smiled up at him. He dropped to his knees, shaking his head.

"What's the matter, big boy?"

"Nothin'." He kept looking at her.

"You sure?"

He shrugged. "Something tells me you've been here before."

She reached up and put her arm around his neck. "Now what would put an idea like that in your head?"

"Not a thing." He laughed. "Not a goddamn thing." He lay down beside her and smothered her with a kiss. His hand went around her back, and he struggled with a button on the back of her dress until it finally popped off.

"I'll do it." She sat up and quickly undid the buttons.

"You sure it's okay?" Sid rested his head in his hand, suddenly remembering Foley's admonitions about the Puget debs.

"Don't worry." Lynette patted him on the cheek. "I'll still respect you afterward." In one fluid movement she pulled the dress over her head, leaving Sid gaping at her huge breasts.

"Heavenly days," he muttered, then buried his face between them. After a moment he came up for air. "You're a crazy girl, you know that?"

"Um-hm." She started on the buttons of his shirt.

"You'll respect me. That's great. But what I meant..."

"I know what you meant." She kissed him roughly. "And I told you, I'm on the pill. Don't worry, Sid. Just do it." She lay back on the blanket.

"You're sure in some kind of hurry."

"That last ferry's at midnight. I don't get home, there's hell to pay."

Sid undid his buckle and slid down his pants. "I'll do my best to oblige you, ma'am."

At first Zack thought he was going to lose his mind, or at least lose control, but at the last minute he caught himself and regained some of his detachment. Paula lay beneath him, her eyes closed, her perfect littly body undulating slowly as Zack fought to keep his cool. At least he had one thing for which he could be grateful to Byron's whores: they had made a point of teaching him how to be a good lover, a patient one. He almost laughed thinking of the one who told him, "First rule for soldier: never shoot gun before battle starts." That was a tall order to follow after what he'd been through for the last month, but he just let his mind drift off and think about other things for a while. Thinking about Foley was enough to slow anyone down, and thinking about a pregnant Puget deb nearly brought Zack to a halt.

"You okay?" Paula gasped.

"Are you, uh, is it safe for me to..."

"Of course," she said. "I would've said something otherwise. Really. The last thing I want is to get pregnant." She sounded so sincere it was hard not to believe her. But his judgment was off. He should have asked her before now.

"Just to be safe," he said, "I think I'll..."

"Zack Mayo!" She slapped him gently on the behind. "If you pull out I'll kill you."

"I know what you mean." He began to move slowly.

"I'm a Catholic," she said. "Don't you think I know the cycles of my body?"

"I believe you," he said. "I believe you." He lost his detachment, then his composure, then he closed his eyes and floated in a soft blue world, listening to the deep gasps of the woman beneath him and the gentle ebb and flow of the surf on the beach.

"Oooo-wee!" Sid crowed, smiling at himself and Zack in the latrine mirror. "Talk shit to me."

"I think you're talkin' shit to yourself." Zack smiled back, then began brushing his teeth.

"Could you believe those girls?"

Zack nodded. Actually, he couldn't believe them, not Paula anyway. Still, he didn't want to say anything too serious. Christ, he didn't want to feel it either. "Nellie's Nymphos," he gurgled, a large gob of toothpaste and saliva splattering in the sink.

"Jesus!" Sid howled. "That Lynette was something else."

"She *was* something else," Zack echoed.

"I rode her hard and put her up wet." Sid saluted himself in the mirror.

"You did your duty as an officer and a gentleman," Zack said.

"I can't believe how easy it was. I mean..."

"I know," Zack said. "Privilege of rank, my friend."

"You mean you don't think she loved me for myself?"

Zack laughed, wiped his mouth, then shadowboxed with his reflection in the mirror. "Look out, Foley!" he yelled. "I'm ready to take you on for another week."

Sid punched Zack in the arm. "Just thinkin' about next weekend's gonna get me through." Again he saluted himself. "Batteries recharged, sir!" he bellowed. "Ready for all the shit you got, sir!" He put his arm around Zack, and the two candidates laughed all the way to their room.

Lynette came close to running the Falcon off the road three times, but she made it to the ferry thirty seconds before it pulled out for Port Angeles. "One of these nights," Paula said, "you're either going to get us killed or miss the ferry. Then our parents'll kill us."

"You shouldn't make your moments of passion so long," Lynette said.

"It might be worth missing the ferry after all."

"To hell with our folks anyway. One of these nights I just might head south. Forget about coming back to this place for twenty years or so."

Paula nodded, looking out on the black water. "Let's get out." She opened the door and stepped onto the deck.

The girls walked to the railing and stood

there for a moment, saying nothing. Lynette drummed her fingernails on the old wood and finally elbowed Paula in the ribs. "Well, if you're not going to ask, I will. How was it?"

Paula smiled down at the water. "Great."

"Great?"

"That's what I said."

"Details, Pokrif. From what I saw he had an incredible body."

"You saw right. Mmmmm."

"Well, what did he do? I mean, did he do anything different?"

"Everything was different."

"But in what ways?"

Paula felt suddenly invaded, and she looked up at her friend and gave an irritated shrug. It was one of the first times she had ever felt private about an evening's pleasure, but there was no denying the feeling now. She just didn't want to talk about it.

"Did you, uh, come?"

Paula just smiled and looked away, knowing Lynette was dying of envy. She had never experienced that particular pleasure.

"How'd it go with you guys?" Paula asked. It was the best way to get the conversation away from herself.

Lynette shrugged. "Big Sid popped off in somewhere between two and three seconds. Then he had the nerve to say, 'Did you make it too, sweetheart?'"

Paula couldn't help laughing. "Probably his first time in a while."

"Well, I really like him, Paula. And I think he's the kind of guy who's going to make it."

"I hope so."

"Oh, he will. He comes from a family of pilots."

"That's good."

"How about Zack?"

"I think he'll make it too."

"I mean, where's he from? What's his family like?"

Paula shook her head. "He was pretty vague about it."

"Did you see his tattoo?"

Paula nodded. "What do you say we get back in the car? I just want to sit down."

"Fine," Lynette said. "Exercise is tiring."

They sat in silence for the rest of the ride across the sound. Maybe Zack didn't come from a family of fliers, Paula thought. From the way he talked it sounded as if he'd knocked around a lot, probably making most of his way by himself. Well, there was nothing wrong with that. It even increased her admiration for him to think of his doing things on his own. All the guys with tattoos that she knew still hadn't left Port Angeles. She saw a few of them lounging in front of Tim's, a local hangout on their route home. A couple of the guys whistled at Lynette's old Falcon. She responded with the finger and a heavy foot on the accelerator.

"Christ," Lynette said. "And they wonder why we go chasing these future pilots."

"The worst part of being a deb is the ride home," Paula said, almost to herself.

"Maybe Sid'll change all that." Lynette was perpetually hopeful.

"He ask you out for next weekend?"

Lynette shook her head. "But I told him I'd be at the Town Tavern next Saturday night. I think he'll probably be there. How about Zack?"

"I told him the same thing, but he didn't seem anxious to commit himself."

"Fifth week's supposed to be the roughest," Lynette said.

"I think come Wednesday, Zack's gonna wish he took my phone number."

"You hope."

"He'll show Saturday," Paula said. "I know it. I'd even bet my paycheck on it."

"Let's both hang onto our money." Lynette stopped the car in front of Paula's house. "Just in case we have to buy our own beer on Saturday."

"Good idea." Paula opened the door, and Lynette gave her arm a friendly squeeze.

"See you in church tomorrow."

"Amen." Paula got out and stood in the street while Lynette drove away. She then turned and faced the clapboard house on its concrete blocks, hoping she could sneak to bed without a scene. She walked gingerly up the walk, slid the key into the lock, then opened the door with the stealth and caution of a burglar. She tiptoed across the living room and was about to make her move down the hallway when her father's voice boomed out from the bedroom, "Paula, come in here."

She jumped, then exhaled with exasperation

and shook her head. The guy could hear her coming in even if he was passed out in a drunken stupor. But if she ever wanted to talk to him about something, he was stone deaf.

She opened the door and stepped into the darkened room. Suddenly the table lamp went on like a police interrogation light, and Joe Pokrifki rose up in the bed to a sitting position, his hairy chest hanging over the blanket. "Come over here," he snapped. "I want to look at you."

Paula stayed by the door. "I'm sorry I'm late, but Mrs. Rufferwell asked us to help with the cleanup, and..."

"I said, come here!"

She took two steps forward and stopped again. "Daddy, I don't want to get into anything with you tonight. I'm tired and I..."

"Tired from what?" Joe sneered.

"Joe!" Esther Pokrifki rolled over and stared at her husband.

Joe ignored his wife. "Come over here where I can see you," he said to Paula.

She took another couple of tentative steps forward. "Please, Daddy."

He sneered at her. "Look at that sand. You got enough sand on that dress to start your own beach."

She stared at him, saying nothing.

He studied her more closely, then pointed his finger. "And what's that wet place on your dress?"

She didn't even bother to look. She glanced at her mother, who had folded her arms on her chest and was staring despondently at the bedspread, probably lost in her own memories. "I don't know what it is," Paula said.

"Sure."

"Probably something from the cleanup. It could be anything."

Joe Pokrifki rolled his eyes heavenward. "But you knew right off what I was talking about, didn't you, Paula! Did you let that boy..."

"Enough!" she shouted. "Don't you dare ask me that question." She took a deep breath, fighting back her tears of rage. Before he could respond she said, "I'm an adult, and you got no right to push your nose into my affairs like that!"

"Is that right?"

"Yeah, that's right."

Joe pointed his finger at her once again. "Well, young lady, let me tell you something. As long as you live in this house you live by my rules! Besides, you should be dating local boys."

"Not a chance!" Paula nearly exploded with laughter. "There's nobody in this town doing anything with his life except what his father did, which is nothing."

"There's worse things than working for a living," Joe said.

"Yeah? Well, if I can't have better than what's around here, I'd rather be dead!"

"I don't know," Joe muttered. "Sometimes I just don't know what's wrong with everybody"

"Why can't I try to make a better life for myself? What in the hell's so wrong with that?"

Joe shook his head. "Do you honestly think

you'll find a boy in that, uh, that officer's school who's serious about marriage?"

Paula hesitated for a moment, afraid to answer, afraid to even think about it.

"'Cause if you do, you're dumber than I thought." He nodded as though he were full of deep wisdom. "All you'll ever get from their kind is pregnant." Esther looked up and glared at Joe.

"Nothing like that is ever gonna happen to me!" She knew she could hold back her tears no longer, so she turned and fled the room. In the hallway she gasped, then leaned against the wall and covered her mouth with her hands. A terrible silence filled the house, then she heard her father say, almost in a whisper, "Esther, do you think she's using, uh, birth control?"

"Yes, Joe." Paula was surprised at her mother's matter-of-fact tone.

"When did this happen?" Joe asked.

"A long time ago," Esther told him.

Paula walked down the hallway and entered her bedroom. She knew her two younger sisters were awake, but she'd be damned if she was going to talk to them tonight. She didn't even bother turning on her table lamp. She took off her dress and stuffed it under the bed, pulled her pajamas out from under her pillow and put them on. She slid beneath the blankets, lying on her stomach with her arms folded beneath her chest. She wanted to let go and sob like a baby, but because she had no privacy she held her anguish in. I've got to get out of here, she thought. I'm going to die if I don't.

* * *

Nothing was said at breakfast about the
night before. Just one more argument swept
under the rug, unresolved. Instead, the family
ate in silence, Joe Pokrifki lost in the sports
page. Why not, Paula thought. There was no
resolving their differences anyway. She tried
not to think about Zack too much; but she
couldn't help it, and all the way to church, in
the backseat of Joe's Olds Cutlass, she kept
dreaming about next Saturday night when she
would see Zack again. As they pulled up in front
of the church she saw Lynette's three brothers
piling out of the bed of the family pickup; then
Lynette and her gaunt mother climbed down
from the cab. Paula flashed Lynette a suppor-
tive smile and received one in return; then she
trudged up the concrete steps.

6

The taste of freedom was what made the fifth
week harder. The bullshit ration wasn't much
higher than usual, but being out in the world
and experiencing its pleasures made the ration
harder to swallow. Zack saw this right away
and made the necessary adjustments. He was
glad he hadn't taken Paula's phone number,
and although he would occasionally find himself lusting for her body, he fought any anticipation of seeing her again. If he got to Saturday
and she was there, fine. The important thing
was to get to Saturday without fucking up.
Then, if she wasn't there, he would still have
himself, and he would be able to find someone
else. It made him sick to see Topper Daniels
mooning at the phone, acting as though the
broad who had made it with him was more important than the program. Well, maybe Topper

had better things to go back to in civilian life. But for Zack the program was the only thing that mattered. The rest of it could wait.

He shaved another two seconds off his time on the obstacle course and moved up to eighteenth in aerodynamics, passing Sadlier and getting the extra notch when Benson flunked a test and D.O.R.'d. Benson was the tenth member of the class to drop out, and Zack figured that there wouldn't be too many more. If you could make it this far, you could probably make it all the way. From now on, it would take some special incident to push someone over the edge. But he didn't relax his mental attitude. Special incidents took up a lot of space in the world, and they screwed up plenty of people's lives.

On Friday they went over to the old blimp hangar for a taste of something new—nobody bothered telling them what. Foley didn't even escort them. Instead, another noncom led them into the dark, cavernous building where they took seats around what looked like a boxing ring. When all the candidates were seated, the lights suddenly went on above the ring, and the dark figure standing in the center turned out to be Sergeant Foley. He was dressed in a pair of worn, faded, black pajamas. His legs were spread, and his arms were crossed on his chest. He looked as though he had achieved total detachment from the human condition.

"Look at Foley!" Zack whispered.

"Shhh!" Sid seemed frightened.

"Can you believe it?" Zack said.

Casey gave Zack a strange look.

"Something else, huh, Casey?"

Casey looked at Foley, then back at Zack. "The presence of death is something else. He brought it in here with him." She seemed absolutely serious.

"I am the base martial arts instructor," Foley said. He paused for a moment to let it sink in. "So those of you in zero eight must desist from thinking of me as their drill instructor for the next sixty minutes." He gave them his most evil grin. "Try thinking of me as, um, the enemy." He began to turn away, then faced them again as though with an afterthought. "Incidentally, children"—he ran the backs of his hands over his outfit—"I am wearing the uniform of a Viet Cong foot soldier that I killed with these." He held up his hands and turned them over several times. "Hand-to-hand in the red clay of Plei Me, in what used to be South Vietnam. I must've been just about the age of you all, maybe a little younger. Now I'd like a volunteer. How about you, Daniels?" He gave the candidate a friendly grin.

Topper stood up, looking terrified. Sid patted him on the back. "Go put him in the hospital, kid."

"He can't touch me," Topper muttered. "That's the law." He climbed up onto the elevated mat, Foley smiling all the while.

"Hello, pussy." Foley's face suddenly turned cold. "How bad do you want to *survive?*"

Topper stared at him for a moment, then stammered, "Sir, this officer candidate doesn't understand what the drill instructor means, sir."

Foley sneered and shook his head. "Well, let me just see if I can improve your comprehension."

A groan went up from the crowd as Foley leaped on Topper, pulled him down on the mat and came up on top of him, the candidate's throat between the drill instructor's thumb and forefinger.

"Jesus!" Casey muttered.

"He's scarin' him more than hurtin' him," Zack said.

Foley glared at Topper with death in his eyes. "Do you want to survive bad enough to stop me, pussy?"

Topper gagged, saying nothing.

"Or are you relying on my generosity and love of humanity to stop me from killing you?"

Topper's eyes were bugged out in horror. "Please," he pleaded. "No! I can't breathe!"

Foley exploded with an evil laugh.

Sid and Perryman came to their feet and seemed about to climb on the mat when Topper began to fight back. The other candidates cheered him on, and he finally summoned enough survival instinct to wrestle Foley's hand from his throat. He then rolled to the side, holding his throat and gagging. Foley stood up and stared at him with contempt. "Get out of my sight."

Topper nodded and quickly scurried off the mat, certainly not wanting to risk another encounter with mad Foley. The D.I. swaggered to the edge of the mat, sat down, and began putting foam safety-kick pads on his feet. He was obviously pleased at the fear he had struck into his audience. "I know you all think I was a little hard on your classmate," he said. "But if you think that was something, you just wait till you get shot down behind enemy lines." His eyes swept them all. "Yeah, chew on that one awhile. Then remember that about all you're gonna have between you and that P.O.W. camp is what you assholes learn from me!" He paused to let his words sink in, then gave his candidates an ingratiating smile. "Okay, worms. Now that I've got your attention, we can begin."

"Could you believe that shit?" Perryman said as the candidates trudged up the stairs to their rooms. "I ain't never seen nothin' like that."

"He was something else," Sid said.

"You're tellin' me." Topper Daniels stroked his throat and shook his head.

Sid patted him on that back. "I just wonder if there's anything about soldiering Foley doesn't know."

"He probably has trouble with personal relationships," Zack said, almost laughing. "Distinct lack of warmth."

"He's probably pretty good with a whip, though," Sid said.

Perryman nodded. "And clothespins."

"He scared the shit out of me," Topper said. "Almost, anyway."

"He ain't that much," Zack said.

The other three stopped and looked at him.

"Shit!" Perryman said. "I bet he could take your head off with one of those leaping crescent kicks."

"Not if I ducked," Zack said.

Sid snorted. "You'd have to have goddamn good reflexes for that."

"Or I could shoot him."

"Come on, Mayo," Topper said. "I've never seen anything like that."

"I have." Zack suddenly crouched, let out a fearsome yell, spun around twice, and planted his foot gently against Sid's behind.

"You're nuts," Sid said. "You really know how to do that shit?"

Zack spread his palms. "I'm a gentleman, Candidate Worley." He pushed his roommate down the hall. "I would've kicked you in the balls, but I want you to have a good time Saturday night."

"Amen, brother." Sid let out a rebel yell as he entered the room.

"You guys are a couple of basket cases," Perryman said.

Maybe they were all basket cases, Zack thought later that night. He lay in bed listening to Perryman snore while Sid kept muttering "Yes, sir, yes, sir," over and over again. Topper breathed erratically, occasionally letting out little whimpering moans. Zack guessed he had had a pretty tough day. Maybe his girlfriend would shape him up tomorrow night. Zack dozed briefly, dreaming of Paula showing up at Byron's flophouse with a swollen belly and a bouquet of wilted roses. He awoke to a hissing noise. He opened his eyes to see Topper standing at the sink, taking a leak. "Topper! What the fuck are you doing?"

Topper gave a guilty start, and Zack was surprised he didn't pee all over the wall. "Takin' a whiz."

"You ever heard of the goddamn toilet? I just cleaned that sink this morning."

Topper turned, and in the moonlight flooding through the window his face looked like a ghost's. "I'm afraid to go out there, Zack. I know Foley'll catch me. He sleeps in the head, you know."

"Oh, Jesus!" Zack lay back and stared at the ceiling. He turned on his side once more. "He doesn't sleep in the head, man. He just says those things to make you uptight so you'll fuck up. I guess he's gettin' to you."

"I don't know what I'm doing here, Zack. I just don't know."

"Go to sleep, Topper. Now ain't the time for this."

Topper shook his head. "I guess I saw a chance to do something flashy. But I didn't think it out, not totally."

"I don't have time to listen to this," Zack whispered. "You want out, you go tell Foley. Now go to sleep." He rolled on his back and closed his eyes, fully awake. It was at least two minutes before he heard Topper shuffle over to his bed and climb in with a weary sigh. Basket case wasn't the word for it, he thought.

* * *

The Town Tavern would have won no awards for its decor, and it was not the friendliest place around. "These debs know how to pick 'em, don't they?" Zack said, then sipped at his beer and eyed the six hostile townies sitting around the pool table where two of their partners played.

"Yeah," Sid replied. "But I reckon we do look pretty out of place in these uniforms." Their dress whites provided quite a contrast to the Levi's and sweatshirts of the locals.

"Bartender," Zack said as the fat man in his lumberjack shirt walked past.

The man stopped and looked at him, saying nothing.

"Couple more beers here."

The bartender walked to the cooler, pulled out two bottles of Bud, brought them to the candidates, and set them rudely on the bar. "That'll be two bucks."

Sid gave him a big grin. "Could we run a tab?"

"No."

Sid shrugged at Zack. "We can't run a tab." He dropped two singles on the bar, and the bartender crumpled them in his fat hand before moving down to the cash register.

"Nice hospitable folks," Sid said. He let out a horny groan and looked at the door. "Lynette, you'd better get here soon, or I'm gonna have to start lifting me some cars."

"I don't believe you." Zack took a long pull at his bottle. "One date and you're pussy-whipped."

"Don't give me no shit, Mayo-naise. I didn't hear any complaints from you when I suggested we come here." He looked at the door again. "I hope she comes."

"She'll come."

"What makes you think so?"

"'Cause you're a rich socialite Okie. You're a big catch around here."

"Shee-it!" Sid said. "Get off my case, Mayo! I didn't grow up rich."

Zack waved his hand in dismissal. "You were an officer's kid. That's plenty rich enough for me."

"Well, how about you?"

"That's some story, believe me."

"Don't be so damn mysterious," Sid said. "I ain't no broad. Just tell me."

Zack took another drink, looked at the floor, then back at Sid. "Well, for starters, I lived for six years above the raunchiest whorehouse in the Philippine Islands."

"You're shittin' me."

"Ay, palequero," Zack said in his best pidgin English. "You wanee number one girl? Never *hochi* in the P.I. you findee mama-san so pretty like me. *Ay, mestizo,* wha you say? Short time, long time, only ten dollars."

Sid started to laugh, then nudged Zack and pointed to the girls as they came through the door. "You can tell me more about that later."

"Yeah." When Zack saw Paula in her light summer dress, he remembered why he had come to this dive. Both girls cut a path through the gawking townies and glided right into the arms of Sid and Zack, then kissed them gluttonously for half a minute.

"I think we're making some of the locals jealous," Zack said.

"Who cares?" Paula kissed him again, then drew back. "Mmmmm," she moaned. "Now I remember. Mayo the Wop." She gave him a big smile. "Gee, I'm glad you're here. I've been looking forward to this all week."

"Me too," Zack said. He kissed her again. Christ, it was good to see her.

"What would you girls like to do?" Sid asked. "Want to stick around here for a little, or might I suggest another plan?"

"Like pick up some booze and go to a motel?" Lynette said.

Sid nodded. "Or we could do that. Yeah."

"I vote for the motel," Paula said.

Zack slid off the barstool and grabbed Paula's arm. "My kind of group!"

The four of them linked arms and started for the door. Just as they were about to go out, one of the townies stepped to the side and jostled Zack, then tried to pretend it was the other way around. "Hey, make way for the warmongers," he said.

"You tell 'em, Troy," one of the others said.

Zack turned around and faced him. Troy was a couple of inches taller and probably outweighed him by twenty pounds. "What'd you call us?" Zack asked.

"I called you a warmonger. Ain't that what you are?"

Zack eyed Troy for a moment, then smiled, turned, and walked out. The locals followed him outside, and after a moment Troy jogged past him, stopped, turned, and planted himself between Zack and Lynette's Falcon. "Hey, let me ask you something," Troy said.

Zack shook his head and sighed. "What do you want to know?"

"Hey, Zack," Sid said. "Don't get us into anything. Foley'll kill us, you know he will."

Zack put up his hand to shush Sid. He knew that this one was going to be tough to get out of. He gave a quick look at Troy's scuzzy partners as they gathered around. He noticed a frightened look on Paula's face, but Lynette seemed excited, even turned on.

"You guys," Troy said, "you come here for a few months, you rich college boys struttin' around in your ice cream suits like you owned the goddamn place, taking our best women. Who do you think gets left holdin' the bag after you're off flying around the world?"

"It ain't that way," Zack said.

"It ain't, huh?" Zack could feel Troy's anger, and he figured he'd probably feel the same way if he were in Troy's position.

Zack put up his hands to indicate he didn't want any trouble. "Hey, pard, why don't you go back inside and cool off." He turned away from Troy and pushed his way out of the circle, continuing what was becoming an odyssey to Lynette's car.

"Hey!" Troy yelled. "I'm not finished with you, sailor boy!" He charged after Zack and knocked his cap off, then jumped in front of him and gave a little laugh. "Come on, punk." Troy raised his fists.

The fight lasted fifteen seconds, and five of those were spent by Zack staring at Troy as he set the coil within himself. Then he crouched, came up, and before Troy could move his hands Zack had hit him in the face with a left and a right. Troy stood there stunned, unable to react as Zack went into a low roundhouse spin. It seemed as if Zack were moving in slow motion, but all of a sudden his foot came flying through the air like an artillery projectile and landed smack dab in the middle of Troy's face. A collective groan went up from the townies as their hero crumpled to the ground, both his nostrils gushing blood. Zack quickly surveyed the others and knew immediately that none of them was about to challenge him. Most of them looked as if they hadn't seen fighting like that in their lives. Zack flashed on himself when he was thirteen years old, lying in the alley in the Philippines, then he grabbed Paula's arm and led her to the car. He was grateful that she said nothing.

"God!" Lynette crowed as they got to the car. "That's one of the most amazing things I've ever seen. Did you see that guy's nose?"

Zack whirled and faced her. "For Christ's sake, Lynette. Could you just keep your mouth shut until we get to the motel?"

"I..."

"Would you do that for me? Please!" Zack climbed into the car.

"Well, excuse me for livin'." Lynette said.

"Just drive, honey." Sid gently pushed her into the car, then gave Zack a sympathetic look. Zack nodded in acknowledgment before dropping his eyes and staring at the floor.

They stopped at a liquor store and got two pints of rum and some mix, then checked into rooms at the Tides Inn Motel. Zack wished he had his motorcycle; he would have liked nothing better than to be blasting down the highway at about a hundred miles per hour. Instead, he sat on the bed and stared at the wall, doing some serious drinking straight from the bottle. Paula had mixed herself a drink, spent some time in the easy chair, a few minutes looking out the window, and she had even thumbed through the Gideon Bible. Zack couldn't help it; he just couldn't think of anything to say. She walked around the bed and stared at him. "You want a back rub?"

He said nothing.

"It might make you feel better."

He took another swig of rum as she climbed on the bed and tried to position herself behind him. When she touched him he pulled away. "Come on!" he said.

"Oh, Jesus," she said. "What's wrong?"

"The fight. What did you think?"

She shrugged. "It's over."

He shook his head. "I shouldn't've done it. I should've walked the hell away from there."

"He didn't give you much choice."

"There's always a choice." There was always a choice between being a lowlife or not.

Paula got off the bed and straightened her dress. "Where'd you learn to fight like that?"

"I don't feel like talking!" Zack snapped. "If you don't mind."

"Have it your way." She started for the door, then turned around. "Opening up just a little wouldn't kill you, you know."

Zack looked up as she got to the door. "You want me to fuck you?" he said.

She turned and looked at him, wondering if she had heard correctly.

"Is that it?" he said. He gave her a silly smile and patted the bed beside him. "Okay, come here. Take your clothes off. Get into bed. I'll take care of you."

"Where the hell is that coming from?" Her lower lip quivered, then tightened with anger. "I wouldn't fuck you now if my life depended on it."

"Forget it." Zack took another pull on the pint. "Just get out of here."

"I don't know who the hell you think you're talkin' to," she said. "I ain't some whore you brought here!" She lowered her head and looked at the floor. "I've just been trying to be your friend, and you end up treating me like shit!"

I feel like shit, he thought. He gave her as hard a look as he could. "Be a friend. Leave."

She eyed him hatefully for a moment before opening the door, then said, "You got no manners and you never tell the truth! You're nothin' special. Can't you even look at me?"

He glanced up from the bedspread. It seemed silly, but she was awfully pretty when she was mad.

"If you ask me," she said, "you got no chance at all of becoming an officer."

He suddenly shot off the bed, hardly knowing why. She flinched as he came toward her, and he slowed down and stopped a couple of feet away. She looked very confused. He reached out with one hand and closed the door. Then he bent over and kissed her as gently as he knew how. He opened his eyes to see hers open too, confused. He kissed again, and slowly she responded. After a moment he pulled away and said, "I'm sorry. Please don't leave me alone tonight."

"I won't," she whispered. "Just don't go away from me."

"I'm with you," he said. "I'm staying." He kissed her again and began backing slowly toward the bed.

He awoke to the smell of bacon and eggs— the best possible smell on a Sunday morning— and the sound of something sizzling in a pan. For a moment he thought he was dreaming, then he opened his eyes and saw Paula in the kitchenette wearing jeans and a halter top, a spatula in her right hand. She gave him an absolutely lovely smile. "Morning, sleepy head."

"You stayed after all."

She shook her head. "Wrong. Since I last saw you I've driven a hundred miles, told a hundred lies, and said a hundred Hail Marys."

"Long night."

She nodded. "You hungry?"

"I'm starving." He jumped out of bed and slid into his boxer shorts. As he walked toward the rickety table where Paula had put the silverware, he noticed a small bunch of wildflowers in a water glass. "Nice," he said.

"We aim to please." She put the steaming plate on the table.

Zack sat down and wolfed a few bites, then looked up to see Paula staring at him wistfully. He swallowed what was in his mouth and smiled at her. "This is great."

"I thought you'd like it."

"Paula, I never try to fool anybody about who I am or what I want."

She nodded.

"So if even in the back of your..."

"I know who you are," she said. "And I know what you want. At least I think I do."

"What do *you* want, Paula? What do you really want?"

"To have a good time with you until you have to go."

"That's it?" But he already knew that that was never it. But he didn't say anything when she nodded and turned away quickly. Well, he thought, at least it's been said. At least on the surface no one's fooling anyone. He downed half a cup of coffee, then vacuumed up what remained of his breakfast as though Foley were hovering above him, waiting to drum him out of the program if he spent too long at table. "That's fantastic," he said.

Paula came over and refilled his coffee cup. He reached up and undid her halter and kissed her gently on each breast. "Last night was fantastic too."

She shrugged. "Wasn't bad."

He laughed. "How're Sid and Lynette?"

"They oughta be coming through the wall any minute. I guess he had more staying power last night."

"That's my man." He kissed her breasts again, then nestled his head against them. He could have stayed that way all morning.

She watched him for a moment, feeling more womanly power than she could remember. "Zack?"

"Hm?"

"Am I your fantasy?"

He laughed softly against her skin.

"Zack, I dare you not to fall in love with me."

He pulled back and gave her a curious look.

"Don't worry," she said. "I ain't gonna get serious with you. No way. But how can you resist me? I'm like candy."

He nodded. "You're better than candy."

"You better watch out."

"Why's that?"

"It's gonna be hard to get enough of me."

"Is that right?" He pulled her down in his lap, cupping her firm breast in his hand.

"I'm serious."

"Gettin' cocky, aren't you?" Zack said. "Huh, you little Polack?"

She just stared at him with her green eyes.

"Don't go gettin' feisty on me, now." He pulled her to him and kissed her long and deeply. He was suddenly awash in strange and fearful feelings, and he pulled away from her, almost in panic. She looked at him until he turned away.

"Zack?"

"Yeah." He tried to make it matter-of-fact.

"What do you do when you're through with a girl?"

"Meaning?"

"Meaning, do you say something, or do you just disappear?"

"That's a good one." He thought back on the girls he had known, girls in the Philippines, on college campuses, on the road. Finally, he told Paula the truth. "I've never had a girl." He snorted as the fact sunk in. "I mean, uh, you know what I mean?"

"Uh-huh." She stroked his hair. "I know just what you mean."

"Yeah." There really wasn't anything more to say. "Hey, I forgot to thank you for the breakfast."

"Any time, sailor boy." She folded her hands behind his neck. "Now, do you think you could see your way clear to carrying me over to that bed?"

"You're too much, you know that?" He stood up with her cradled in his arms. "You're too goddamn much." He walked across the room and laid her gently on the bed.

"You ain't seen nothin' yet." She pulled him down on top of her.

7

Zack could see right away that the whole key to the Dilbert Dunker was keeping your cool. Too much anticipation, too much panic, and it would be all over. Meant to simulate the cockpit of an aircraft, the orange, cagelike Dunker ran down a set of tracks from the rafters, crashed into the pool below, then submerged while turning somersaults. Once the Dunker stopped, the prospective pilot was to undo his harness, get out of the cage, and swim to the surface. Easy if you didn't panic, Zack thought, wondering why they hadn't put a couple of sharks into the pool just to make things a little more interesting.

"I don't know about this," Sid whispered as the Dunker was pulled into the rafters and Della Serra climbed in.

"I thought you said it was easy."

"That's what my father and brother said. Looks a little scary up close."

Zack gave him a little grin. "Just think of Lynette on the surface of the water. You'll get out."

"Amen, brother." Sid shook his head. "Sweet weekend, huh?"

"Aren't they all," Zack said.

Della Serra gave the instructor the thumbs up, and the Dunker tore down the rails and crashed into the water, then quickly sank beneath the surface.

"Come on, D.S." Sid said.

The distorted Dunker spun in the water, sending a rush of bubbles to the surface.

Foley hovered at the side of the pool, looking down. Across from him stood an instructor wearing fins and a mask, ready to assist any candidate who got in trouble.

The Dunker stopped spinning, and the surface of the pool grew calmer. The silence was amazing.

Nothing seemed to be happening down below. "Jesus," Sid muttered, and soon a few of the other candidates began to mumble and groan. Foley looked across at the instructor. The instructor looked up at his boss near the ceiling.

Another ten seconds went past, and still Della Serra hadn't appeared. "Okay," the instructor near the ceiling hollered, and the man at poolside immediately dove into the water.

The candidates began to make more noise. "Come on, man!" Sid said.

"Don't worry." Zack held out his hand. "That's what the guy's trained for. He'll bring him up."

The group grew silent once again, and in what seemed like an endless five seconds, the instructor brought Della Serra to the surface. The candidate gasped loudly, then sucked in the air. The instructor near the ceiling gave him the thumbs down.

Della Serra vomited into the gutter of the pool. When he looked up, Foley was standing there, a pleasant smile on his face. "Back in line, Sweet Pea. That was totally unsatisfactory."

Della Serra looked at him, saying nothing.

"Unless, of course, you'd like to D.O.R." Foley's smile was even more kind.

"No, sir!" Della Serra gasped, then pulled himself out of the pool. He shook himself off like a dog and headed for the end of the line. Walters, Jordan, and Gonzales went before Zack, and each struggled to the surface looking as if he had come face to face with the Loch Ness monster.

When Zack's turn came, he climbed into the cage totally focused. First of all, let the damn thing stop; then watch the direction of the air bubbles while you're unbuckling your harness. Then follow the bubbles to the surface. One, two, three. Easy as that. When he was strapped in, he looked down at the water to see Foley grinning up at him.

"Go get 'em, Zack," Sid yelled.

Zack stared back at Foley, then gave the instructor the thumbs up.

The ride to the water was like the first down-hill plunge on a big roller coaster. Zack's chest slammed into the harness as the Dunker impacted against the coaster, and he barely managed to fill his lungs with air before the cage submerged. He got hold of his harness and then hung on, waiting while the machine somersaulted again and again and again. He took a moment to acknowledge that he had no idea in which direction he was pointing, then he opened his eyes, breathed out, and watched his bubbles climb to the surface. He slid out of his harness with ease, vacated the cage, and chased his bubbles up into the air. He broke the water and spun his head around, giving Foley a big grin.

The instructor gave the thumbs up.

"Not bad, Mayo-naise," Foley said. "Not bad at all."

"Thank you, sir." Zack pulled himself out of the pool.

Foley patted him on the back and gave him an odd-looking grin. "You're an exemplary candidate, Mayo."

"Uh, thank you, sir."

Foley nodded. "I'll be lookin' for you to do well at inspection tomorrow."

"I'll do my best, sir."

"Oh, I'm sure you will." Foley pointed to the rafters. "Let's watch your buddy."

"Yes, sir."

Sid rode the Dunker into the water with his cheeks puffed out as though he were playing the trombone. He wasn't under too long, but when he broke the surface there was a look of panic on his face. He swam to the edge, pulled himself up beside Zack, and tried to mask his fear with a cocky grin.

"You okay?" Zack asked.

"Sure," Sid said. He took a deep breath. "I reckon I am, anyway. How'd I look?"

"Like you were born to crash at sea." Zack looked up at the Dunker. "Check the See-gar beev."

Casey actually looked happy as she rode the Dunker down, and it wasn't more than five seconds before she pulled herself up next to Sid and Zack, an exhilarated grin on her face. "Christ," she said. "That was fantastic!"

"Macho woman," Zack said.

"Think they'll let us do it again?" she asked.

"Next time, you get to go one-on-one with Jaws," Zack said.

"Here goes Topper," Sid said.

Topper loooked as if he was about to drop his load as he tentatively got into the cage. "Does this thing hit with the same impact as an actual plane?" he asked the instructor.

The man shook his head. "This ain't nothin' compared to a plane."

Topper finished strapping in.

"Don't forget to watch the bubbles," the instructor said.

Topper nodded, then stared straight ahead.

After a moment the instructor said, "Well?"

"Oh." Topper looked at him, then back at the water. Finally he gave the thumbs up.

"Jesus Christ," Zack muttered as the Dunker hit the water and disappeared.

"What?" Sid said.

"Did you see his face? He was scared shitless."

They watched the bubbles come up, but no Topper followed them. There seemed to be a great deal of activity in the Dunker itself.

"Come on!" Sid said.

"Okay," the instructor hollered, and the diver disappeared into the water.

"He panicked, I know it," Zack said.

"What the hell's happening?" Sid said. There was a flurry of motion and bubbles at the bottom of the pool, but no one was surfacing.

Zack looked up at Foley, and he had never seen more concern on the sergeant's face. A few more seconds ticked off. Foley suddenly dove into the water without even taking off his hat, which floated on the surface next to his swagger stick. The candidates were all on their feet now, groaning and urging Foley on. Who the hell knew what was going on down below? There was nothing but a tangle of bodies beneath a screen of bubbles.

Another instructor appeared at poolside and was about to dive in when Foley's shining head broke the surface. He had the diver in one hand, Topper in the other. The instructor took the diver, who was gasping heavily, but Topper just hung there, lifeless. Sid rushed to pull him out of the pool, and in an instant Foley was beside him. He pushed Topper's stomach twice, causing some water to run out of his mouth, then he covered Topper's lips with his own and began mouth-to-mouth resuscitation.

In less than a minute the candidate began to revive, gasping and panicking all over again. Although Foley's face was stern, he held Topper tenderly so the defeated candidate had room to move and still wouldn't slam his head into the hard tile deck. Gradually Topper came around; his breathing got steady, and he quit flailing at the imaginary water threatening to engulf him. And then a look of great sadness and shame came over his face, and the other candidates returned to their places in line or retreated out of Topper Daniels' angle of vision.

He D.O.R.'d that afternoon, was gone that night, and the next morning, as Zack, Sid, and Perryman hurried to get ready for inspection, Topper's empty locker and rolled mattress served as stark warnings of the possible failure that still awaited them all. Perryman had bumped his belt buckle into the door and was anxiously working on it while Sid and Zack stood at ease beside their lockers. Finally Perryman gave Zack a hopeless look. "I'll never get it polished in time, Zack. Give me a buckle, man."

Zack could already hear Foley going through another room down the hall. "Sorry, man. I can't risk it."

"You'd make it," Perryman said. "He's just starting with the girls."

"Uh-uh."

"Come on, Zack. I gotta see my family. I

couldn't take it if he keeps me here over the weekend."

Zack shook his head. "Sorry, pard."

"Oh, man."

"Anyway, I wouldn't want you to get an honors violation."

Perryman gave him a dirty look, then put away his polishing gear. "Thanks, man."

Zack shrugged.

Sid shook his head and looked away.

"Ten-hut!" Perryman said as Foley strode into the room.

Foley said nothing. Beads of sweat ran down Perryman's face, but Foley only spent about seven seconds on him and his locker before moving on to Sid. He spent even less time with him before nodding and facing Zack. Then he just stared for about fifteen seconds.

Zack was about to say something when Foley said, "Well, Mayo."

"Yes, sir."

Foley gave his ingratiating smile, the one with the killer behind it. "In every class there's a guy who thinks he's smarter than me." He let the words hang for a moment. "In this class it's you, isn't it, Mayo-naise?"

Zack shook his head. "No, sir."

"Oh?" Without even looking up, Foley suddenly raised his left arm. The swagger stick knocked out a piece of fiberboard, and two pairs of boonies and six freshly shined buckles rained down on the floor. Foley never took his eyes off Zack, and the smile never left his face.

Zack eyed his gear, then looked back at

Foley, trying to keep a straight face. The game was up, that much he knew. His heart was thumping and his stomach felt hollow, but he tried to let his face show nothing. If they threw him out, they threw him out. But he wasn't going to break in front of everyone.

"I want your D.O.R," Foley said.

"No, sir."

"I want it, Mayo!"

He shook his head. "You can kick me out, sir, but I'm not quitting."

"Now, Mayo! I want you out now!"

"No, sir!" Zack bellowed. "I'm not quitting."

Foley stared into his eyes for another ten seconds, then looked down at his shoes. "Why don't you hop into your fatigues, Mayo," he said almost gently.

"Yes, sir."

"You know," Foley said, "I was gonna go out this weekend, get drunk, probably get some pussy, abuse the shit out of my body."

"Yes, sir," Zack said.

"But you, Mayo, have saved me from all that. Now I get to stay around here all weekend and help you abuse *your* body. You gettin' my drift, Mayo-naise?"

"I think so, sir."

"You think so!" Foley said. "Believe me, Mayo, before this weekend's over you'll be beggin' me to let you quit." Foley grinned savagely at him. "Now you have your ass outside in five minutes! It belongs to me, Sweet Pea." Foley spun on his heel and left the room.

Zack hesitated for only a moment, feeling

briefly sad that he would miss the weekend with Paula, then he tore off his khakis and began putting on his fatigues. The only thing he could afford to think about was getting through the torture that Foley was cooking up. Sid and Perryman just stood there, staring at him. "You tell the girls hello for me," Zack said.

Sid shook his head. "I'll stay here if you want. Give you some moral support."

"You're nuts too." Perryman began changing his clothes.

"Thanks anyway," Zack said. "But I don't think it would do much good." He forced a little laugh. "You might want to help bury me when it's all over."

"You'll make it. You're a tough son of a bitch."

"As nails." Zack sat on the bed and began lacing up his boonies.

"We'll drink a few beers in your honor."

"Thanks."

"You scared?"

Zack tied one of the boots. "Shitless."

"Well, Mayo," Perryman said. "If you ain't here when I get back, it was nice knowing you."

"Oh, I'll be here." Zack finished his other boot, stood up, and did a poor imitation of a soft-shoe routine. "Off to the slaughter."

"Hang in there, good buddy," Sid said.

Zack raised his fist. "I'll give it my best shot."

Foley ran him for five miles first. Neither the distance nor the pace caused Zack any problems, but he knew it was only the beginning.

"You're lookin' hot, there, Mayo-naise," Foley said as Zack finished the run. "Looks like you could use some cooling off."

Zack said nothing.

"Well?" Foley demanded.

"What, sir?" Zack wheezed.

"Are you hot, Candidate Mayo?"

"A little. Yes, sir!"

"Let's go cool you off then. Double time, harch!"

They ran back to the company area, halting in the middle of the large green lawn. The other candidates were leaving the barracks, and people kept walking past on the sidewalk. Foley looked around for a moment, then turned to Zack and said, "I'll be back in a minute with something nice and cool for y'all."

"Yes, sir," Zack said. "Thank you, sir."

Foley gave him a patronizing smile. "Don't mention it." He walked a few steps, then stopped and turned around. "Double-time in place, harch!" He nodded as Zack began strutting up and down, then turned and walked away.

So far, so good, Zack thought. He still had quite a bit of energy left, and he wasn't taxing himself now. A couple of his classmates gave him the thumbs up as they walked past, and the two children of an officer's wife laughed at him until their mother shut them up. He almost laughed himself. He must have looked pretty damned ridiculous. Maybe someone would think he was a nut-job and call the men in the white coats. A deb walked by and gave him a sour look, and he thought of Paula and her body and how nice it was to be with her. "Forget it," he muttered, then tried to look more serious when he saw Foley coming.

The D.I. had a rifle in one hand and was dragging a hose in the other. "Catch, Mayo." He tossed the rifle at him, and Zack caught it at port arms without losing a stride. "Good, Mayo. Now hold it there and keep on going."

"Yes, sir."

Foley took a drink from the gurgling hose. "Still hot, Mayo?"

"Yes, sir." He was.

Foley sprayed him. "We can't have that. You just keep running in place, and I'll just keep cooling you off."

"Yes, sir." Zack kept it up as Foley walked completely around him a couple of times, dousing him from head to foot. The water actually felt good, and he even managed to get a little in his mouth. But then his boots began to fill up, his uniform got heavy, and soon the ground beneath him was a mucky bog. Every step became harder and harder, and all the time Foley was standing there like a vulture, waiting for Zack to fold. No way, Zack thought. As long as he remained conscious he'd keep at it.

"We need some music, Mayo. What do you say?"

"Whatever you want, sir," Zack gurgled.

"Music, Mayo-naise. And nothing soothes my ears so much as the sound of my own voice. Repeat after me, please." And Foley sang his song in a marching cadence, with Zack repeating every line:

Casey Jones was a son of a bitch.
Drove his train in a thirty-foot ditch.
Came on out with his dick in his hand,
Said, "Listen ladies, I'm a helluva man."
Went to his room and lined up a hundred.
Swore up and down he'd fuck every one.
Fucked ninety-eight till his balls turned blue,
Then he backed off, jacked off, and fucked the
other two.

Twice Zack sucked in water as he tried to sing, and both times he had to sputter and cough before he could start again. By the time they finished he was breathing harder, his arms were getting sore from carrying the rifle, and he was ankle deep in mud. Foley let him go awhile, then said, "Let's head over to the gun emplacements, Mayo-naise. Sun gets real nice over there this time of day."

"Yes, sir."

Foley left him in the mud while he took back the hose, then they started out for the beach. Zack was beginning to wonder how much of this *Foley* could take. The guy must be a sadist. No one would do this if it wasn't fun.

"Take a break, Mayo." Foley stopped by the obstacle course, and Zack did too. He bent over and sucked in the air. "Look over there." Foley pointed to the ten-foot wooden wall where Casey Seeger, dressed in a sweatsuit, was desperately trying to climb all the way up the rope.

She was a quarter of the way from the top when she had to stop and let herself back down. She kicked the wall, then walked over to a chin-up bar and began working on her strength.

"She stayed to do that instead of going on liberty, Mayo."

He said nothing.

"Double-time, harch!"

They started off once again.

"She may not make it through the program, Mayo, but she's got more heart and more character than you'll ever have."

Zack shot him a look.

"That's right, Mayo. Man, I've seen your college record. I haven't even heard of a couple of those schools. Are you one of those people who bought his degree, Mayo?"

"No, sir. It was the hardest thing I ever did, sir. Until this."

They entered the woods, Foley running behind Zack and chuckling softly. "That's a lie, Mayo."

"Sir?" Zack wished he could see the bastard.

"You've been through a lot worse, haven't you?"

Zack glanced back over his shoulder, wondering how much Foley knew.

"Stop eyeballing me, mister!"

Zack faced front again.

"I've looked through your file, Mayo. I've done a little checking, and I know it all. The Navy doesn't like security risks, Mayo. They check up on everyone before they turn a millon-dollar aircraft over to 'em."

Let it come, Zack thought. Just keep putting one foot in front of the other.

"I know about your mother," Foley said. "And I know your father's an alcoholic whore-chaser."

Zack resisted an impulse to whirl around and butt-stroke Foley with the rifle. He ran on.

"Life has dealt you some pretty shitty cards, hasn't it, Mayo?"

"I'm doing okay, sir."

"No, you're not, Mayo. You're failing in the big one, baby, and I don't mean just in here. I mean in life."

They came out of the woods, and Foley moved abreast of Zack on the beach. "I've watched you, man, and you don't mesh. Sure, you grab-ass and joke around, but you don't make friends."

"I've..."

"Not the way other people do. Because it would mean giving something you don't have anymore, something that was beaten out of you a long time ago."

Zack kept his eyes straight ahead. He felt Foley getting to him, and he didn't want to look at the D.I. The fucker knew how to go for the jugular. Or the balls. Or both.

They jogged through the tunnel in silence, and as they got to the steps of the gun emplacement, Foley shouted, "Detail, halt!"

Zack did as he was told, bending over to take a deep breath.

"You stand at attention, boy!"

Zack snapped upright, putting the rifle at the order arms position at his side. It was worse than being at ease, but it was better than running. The gun emplacement was going to be tough, and he needed all the rest he could get.

"Lotta fun, hey, Mayo?"

He said nothing.

Once again the patronizing smile spread across Foley's face. "Want to know why I'm not an officer, Mayo?"

"Yes, sir." He did wonder sometimes.

"Because I have a servile mentality from growing up poor, from always being on the windy side of the baker's window. That's your problem too, Mayo. That's why you don't mesh." Foley gave him a long look. "Because deep down in that bitter little heart of yours, you know that these other boys and girls are better than you."

The words hit Zack like a sledgehammer, but his face didn't show a thing. He kept staring back, right past Foley. Maybe the bastard was right, but Zack was here to show he could better himself, to prove that he was just as good as everyone else.

"Now you double-time up and down those stairs until I tell you to stop. Move!"

Zack moved. And moved and moved and moved.

Foley gave him a break for dinner—ten whole minutes—then took him out behind the barracks and put him through an hour of rifle drills. The physical punishment of all the running had been hard, but there was an irritation that went with constantly changing rifle positions that nearly made Zack throw up his arms

and give Foley his goddamn D.O.R. "Port, arms!
Order, arms! Right shoulder, arms! Left, face!
Order, arms! About, face!" The only thing that
kept Zack going was his knowledge—or maybe
it was just hope—that Foley was just as tired
of this crap as he was. Finally, after a last
"Order, arms!" Foley said, "Dis-missed!"

Zack couldn't believe what he had just heard.
He stood there, staring at his D.I.

"You heard me, Mayo. Get the hell out of
here."

"Yes, sir." Zack handed back the rifle, turned,
and started toward the barracks. He still had
time to meet Paula.

"Oh, Mayo," Foley called.

Zack stopped and turned around. "Yes, sir?"

"You *will* meet me out here at twelve hundred
hours tomorrow."

Zack nodded. "Yes, sir." He turned to leave
again.

"Mayo?"

He faced the D.I. "Yes, sir."

"You *will* be wearing starched fatigues and
spit-shined boots."

"Yes, sir."

"And you *will* have scraped the old wax off
the hallway on your floor, washed it down,
waxed it up, buffed it off, and polished it like
glass."

Zack nodded slowly. There went his night on
the town.

"Am I making myself clear, Mayo-naise?"

"Perfectly, sir!"

Foley smiled. "You can go now, Mayo. You get a good night's rest, ya hear?"

"Yes, sir." Zack spun on his heel and double-timed up the stairs.

He decided to do it all before he went to sleep. No sense screwing around. If he didn't have it done, Foley would run his ass right out of the program. Christ, a coat of wax could change your whole life. Don't take it personally, he told himself.

In his room he discovered that Foley had confiscated all of his spit-shined boonies. Good trick, asshole, Zack thought, looking down at his scarred and mud-caked boonies. It would take him half the night to get them squared away, let alone the goddamn floor. He felt so tired that he had to fight himself from lying down on his bunk for an extended catnap. No way, he thought. I'm gonna do this if I have to stay up till noon.

He went over to the snack bar and got a canteen full of coffee, then came back to the barracks and started in. He scrubbed off his boots, then set them in the window to dry while he scraped the wax off the hallway floor. Then he put a first coat of polish on the boots, enough to bring up a little shine, then let them sit again while he went over the hallway with a scrub brush. He put another coat of polish on the boots, then wet-mopped the hallway twice. While it dried, he polished his boots again— they were beginning to glisten—then he put a coat of wax on the floor. He spit-shined the toe and heel of one boot, buffed the floor, then spit-shined the other boot. As the sun came up, he went down to the latrine and took a shower, then put a towel beneath the buffer and went over the floor again until it was, as Foley had ordered, like glass. Finally, he shaved and put out his starched fatigues, then tumbled into bed. It was zero eight hundred hours.

The charge of quarters woke him at eleven-thirty, and just as Zack finished lacing up his boots, Foley strode into the room. Zack leaped to attention, shouting, "Atten-hut!"

"At ease, Mayo." Foley smiled once again. "Ready for another day of fun, or do you just want to give me your D.O.R. now so we can call off this bullshit?"

"Ready for another day, sir!" He was aching in places he didn't even know he had.

Foley nodded, looking him over. "You look good, Sweet Pea. Nice and fresh. Maybe I didn't give you enough to do yesterday." Foley turned on his heel and left, Zack following. "Hallway looks good too."

"Thank you, sir." He had half-expected Foley to have spread sand all over it or something.

"Your classmates'll be grateful. Too bad you won't be around to see 'em."

Zack followed Foley outside, saying nothing.

Foley lounged in the bleachers by the football field while Zack did twenty laps around the track. He went as slow as he possibly could, both to conserve energy and to loosen up gradually. Lord only knew what was ahead. He couldn't figure whether or not Foley was really serious about breaking him, but to be on the safe side Zack had to assume that he was. Why else go through this bullshit?

The five-mile run was followed by three trips around the obstacle course, a ten-minute lunch, cleaning the grease trap out behind the mess hall, a leisurely double-time out to the gun emplacements, then four trips up and down the weathered stairs. All the time Foley said nothing beyond the simplest orders. Zack's legs felt like tree trunks, and on the fifth climb he stumbled and fell twice. When he got to the top, Foley gave a little shrug. "Okay, Mayo. Take a break."

"Thank you, sir." Zack looked out to sea from the top slab of the bunker, greedily sucking in air. He didn't see how he could take much more of this, but his mind was still firm. *He* wasn't going to quit. Maybe his body would stop or wouldn't do what he was telling it, but his body could decide that on its own. He'd give it all he had.

"Relax, Mayo. Sit down."

"Yes, sir." He knew something was coming, but there was no sense trying to anticipate. He sat down.

"Feel better?"

"Yes, sir."

"Go ahead and lie down."

"This is fine, sir."

"Lie down, worm!" Foley howled. "On your back. And I want your fuckin' feet six fuckin' inches off the fuckin' ground!"

"Yes, sir!" Zack was on his back in an instant, in the desired position.

Foley smiled as though he were Zack's best friend. "Good, Sweet Pea. Real good." He eyed Zack for a moment, then looked out to sea while whistling "The Battle Hymn of the Republic."

Foley didn't even look at him as he whistled through one stanza and the chorus. Zack tried to keep his eyes off the D.I. too, but he couldn't help stealing a glance from time to time. Although the temptation was strong to drop his heels on the ground, Zack wasn't about to do it. Foley would know. Even if he were deaf, dumb, and blind, he'd know.

When Zack's legs began to shake, Foley turned his head and smiled down at him. Son of a bitch, Zack thought, looking past him. Sadistic son of a bitch. He couldn't hold up his legs much longer, and Foley was going to be grinning when his heels touched down. Zack wondered if he could get thrown out of the program for not holding up his legs.

"Hey," Foley said, "what do you say we call off this little charade of yours and knock back a couple of brews over at T.J.'s?"

Zack shook his head.

"Come on, man. You're about as close to being officer material as me."

"Sir," Zack sputtered, "this candidate believes he'd make a good officer, sir!"

Foley guffawed. "No way, Mayo." He bent over until his face was two feet from Zack's. "You don't give a shit about anybody but yourself, and every single one of your classmates knows it."

"No, sir." He bent his knees to ease the shaking. Foley didn't notice.

"Think they'd trust you behind the controls of a plane they have to fly in?"

"Yes, sir."

"Hey, man, I figure you for the kind of guy who'd zip off one day in my F-14 and sell it to the Cubans."

Zack's legs were like lead, his stomach was burning, and he felt suddenly furious at Foley's accusations. "That's not true, sir!" he bellowed. "I love my country."

"Sell it to the Air Force, Mayo." The D.I. kneeled down and put his lips a few inches from Zack's ear. "Let's get down to it. Why would a slick little hustler like you sign up for this kind of abuse?"

Zack's heels touched the ground, but he quickly pulled his legs up. "This candidate wants to fly, sir."

"That's no reason. Everybody wants to fly. My grandmother wants to fly." Foley shook his head. "You going after a job with one of the airlines?"

"The candidate wants to fly jets, sir!" Howling eased the pain a little.

"Why?" Foley demanded. "Because you can do it alone?"

"No, sir!"

"What is it, the kicks? Is that it?"

"I don't want to do something anybody can do." His boots hit the ground, but when Foley looked at them, Zack managed to pull them up again. He felt as if he were going to explode.

Foley stood up and shook his head. "Pity you don't have the character."

"That's not true, sir!" Zack screamed.

"It is!"

"I've changed a lot since I've been here. And I'm gonna make it, sir!"

"Not a fucking chance, asshole." Foley turned his back on him. "I'm throwin' you out of the program."

Zack's legs hit the ground, and he took a deep breath. "You can't do that, sir!" he bellowed.

Foley turned and faced him. "I'm doin' it."

"You can't!" Zack sat up and hugged his knees, fighting back tears. "You can't."

"Why not?"

"'Cause I got nothing else to fall back on. Don't you see?" He could feel the hot tears streaming down his face.

Foley looked down at him, saying nothing.

"I got no other place to go," Zack said. "This is it for me." He wiped his mouth on his sleeve. "And I'm gonna do it, sir!"

Foley stared at him for another long moment, then nodded once. "All right, Mayo. Get on your feet."

For a moment Zack thought he was going to crumple in a heap, but he found that his legs could hold him, and he even managed to take a couple of steps forward. He was trying to figure out what to say to Foley when he heard the yelling and saw the little sailboat. Both he and Foley turned and looked out to sea.

The boat was only fifty yards offshore, and Zack recognized Paula and Lynette right away. The guy with the bag over his head had to be Sid. All three were waving in their direction. Then, with near-military precision, they all turned, dropped their pants, and flashed their bare asses at Zack and Foley. Somewhere Zack found the energy to laugh.

Sid pulled up his pants and turned around. "Don't give up the ship, Mayo!"

"Hang in there, Zack!" Paula yelled.

Lynette held up a clenched fist. "Damn the torpedoes and remember the Tides Inn Motel!"

The three of them were laughing so hard that they nearly capsized the boat.

Foley let Zack watch for a little longer, then prodded him with his swagger stick. "Move it, Mayo!"

"Yes, sir!" Zack started down the steps with a huge grin on his face. He felt as if he could run forever.

"Friends of yours?" Foley asked as they started for the base.

"Uh-huh. Yes, sir," Zack said proudly.

"Maybe there's hope for you after all."

Maybe there was, Zack thought.

The two men jogged the rest of the way in silence.

As a last little treat, Foley let Zack scrub down his own room, and he was just finishing up when Sid and Perryman ambled in, done with their weekend of pleasure. Perryman flashed him a nasty look. "I see you didn't D.O.R., Mayo."

Zack shook his head and grinned. "Actually, they hired me on as a janitor." Perryman walked past, and Zack and Sid shook hands. "Hey, man," Zack said. "Thanks for that little show this afternoon."

"Thought you'd go for that, hoss." Sid gave him a careful looking over. "How was it?"

Zack shrugged. "I'm still here. Aim to stay here."

"Hell, I knew he couldn't break you."

"Oh, he could've," Zack said. "You can break anybody if you go far enough."

"Maybe," Sid said.

"Hey, Mayo," Perryman said.

Zack turned around. Perryman had found the pair of perfectly spit-shined boots and two gleaming belt buckles on his bed. "You didn't have to do this, man."

"I figured I owed it to you."

"Well, thanks."

Zack nodded. "Peace?"

"Peace," Perryman said.

"This place is lookin' shaped up," Sid said.

"Don't you even have a message for me?"

"From who?" Sid walked to his locker and began pulling off his uniform.

"Come on, man."

"Oh, yeah," Sid said. "I almost forgot. She said she was savin' it for you."

"I really missed her."

"She missed you too."

"I tell you, even from fifty yards away it looked good."

"I wouldn't know," Sid said. "I had that goddamn bag over my head."

"Probably the only way you could get laid."

"Tell me about it." Sid pointed at him. "You think you can make it till next weekend?"

"I'm a tough trooper," Zack said. "Besides, what the hell choice do I have?"

"I heard that," Sid said.

Actually, the week went much smoother than Zack had expected. Perhaps the relief of being kept in the program canceled the fatigue from his weekend labors. Whatever the reason, he was full of energy all week, even knocking another two seconds off his time on the obstacle course. Some of the activities he even enjoyed for themselves, not just for what they could get him, and on Friday, during a rifle drill, he experienced the same pride and feeling of belonging that he thought his classmates felt. Still, when the next weekend's liberty came, it didn't take him long to find his way into a double bed at the Tides Inn Motel.

8

He stayed there with Paula most of Saturday
night, getting out once for a late supper and a
couple of drinks. They made love in the middle
of the night and again when they woke up. They
left Sid and Lynette at the motel and went out
for a huge breakfast and a walk on the beach,
but they were back in bed again before noon.
She sat on top of him this time, and they made
love slowly and deliberately, climaxing simultaneously with groans of pleasure that must
have shaken the walls. Zack lay back, fla-
grantly satisfied, and Paula bent over and
wrapped her arms around him. "That was the
greatest," he muttered, pulling the blanket up
over them.

"It sure was," she said.

They lay there for at least fifteen minutes,
and Paula finally broke the intimate silence by
saying, "Want me to get a towel?"

"I'll get it if you want."

"No," she said. "I don't want you to move."

He chuckled. "I don't *want* to move," he said. "And I don't want you to move."

"Quite a predicament."

"But somebody has to move sometime," he said. "I mean, eventually."

She held her hand to her forehead dramatically. "They found them like that, shriveled up from weeks without food or water."

Zack laughed, nearly falling out of the bed. Christ, she was pretty, he thought. He took her face between his hands and kissed her as lovingly as he knew how. Then he pulled back and looked at her. "All week I kept thinking about you guys in that sailboat." He laughed again, slipping out of her this time.

"We were pretty drunk." She lay down beside him. "You know about beer in the hot sun."

"Oh, yeah."

She reached over to the night table, grabbed his cap, and put it on. "You know, sometimes I wish I were one of those girls they're letting in the flight program these days. God, I'd love to fly."

"What's stopping you?" Zack asked.

Paula smiled at him and shook her head as though he should have known better. "I don't care what the magazines say about women and all that. It's just not as easy being a girl, especially from a Catholic family."

"I'll grant you it's harder."

"You don't know the kind of junk I grew up

listening to, about the way women are supposed to think and act."

Zack nodded sympathetically. "But that's no excuse for not going after what you want."

"Who says I'm not going after what I want? My mother's thirty-nine years old, and she still works in that factory. Every time I see her, I know exactly what I *don't* want."

Zack rested his arm on his forehead and stared up at the ceiling. He felt like retreating, like closing up inside himself, then he just decided to tell her. "My old lady swallowed a bottle of pills one day while I was at school." He was amazed at how easily the words came out. He had never said them to anyone before.

"God!" Paula stroked his cheek.

"You know what really got to me?" He was back in their old apartment now, desperately looking from room to room.

Paula shook her head.

"She didn't leave a note. Nothing." Zack doubled his fist and shook it. "I've always hated her for that."

"It must have really hurt."

He said nothing.

"Does it still?"

"Naw." He gave her a hard look. "You're alone in this world no matter what kinda folks or background you had." He punched her gently on the arm. "Once you get that one down, pard, nothing hurts."

She kissed him on each side of his chest, then looked up at him with her impish smile. "I bet most people believe you when you feed 'em that line."

He smiled back. "Where the hell'd you come from, anyway?"

"Dispatched from your guardian angel." She covered his mouth with a kiss.

Zack breezed through the next week's rigors with barely a thought, and when his mind didn't have to be absolutely focused on Foley's shenanigans, it was off into a strange world of its own. He felt uncomfortable about his new feelings toward Paula and worried that perhaps she was getting too close to him. There was still that part of him that mistrusted her because she was a Puget deb, because she had been this route before, and because she would probably be after someone in the class that succeeded his. He was also thinking more about his mother, and twice that week he awoke from dreams in which he was trying to rouse her stiffening body. Then Byron called in the middle of the week to tell Zack that he would be at the air show the next Sunday and would like to spend some time with his son. Sometimes Zack thought it would be better to spend the entire cycle of training in the barracks with no outside interference. That would make life a lot less complicated.

He willingly took the complications on Saturday, getting totally pie-eyed with Paula, Sid, and Lynette while watching a pair of horror movies at a local drive-in. Lynette almost drove her Falcon into the ocean by turning off too soon for the Tides Inn Motel. Zack woke up in a touchy mood on Sunday, growing increasingly morose as the morning wore on. By the time they got to the field where the air show was being held, he realized that it was the thought of seeing Byron that was making him feel so bad. He had told Paula about Byron the day before, but decided that he didn't want her to meet him right away. "Christ, I'm sorry," he said to Paula. "But I don't think I should sit with you this time."

"I understand," she said, a little testy herself. "Maybe we'll see each other after the show." She followed Sid and Lynette into the bleachers.

Zack watched four jets dip low over the field before accelerating while they climbed into the sky. He couldn't wait to get in one himself. Nothing could touch him then. He spotted Byron working on a beer up in the bleachers, took a deep breath, and started up the steps.

Byron finished the beer and gave his son a big smile as Zack sat down next to him.

"How you doin', pard?" Zack asked.

Byron slapped him on the back. "I see you're still here."

Zack nodded, biting his lip to avoid starting an argument. He watched a pair of jets do some loops.

"Still in it for the speed, huh?" Byron said.

Zack shook his head. "It's more than that now."

"I saw that girl you come in with."

Zack shrugged.

"Who is she?"

"Nobody."

"What's that supposed to mean?"

"She's just a girl I've been making it with the last couple of weekends."

Byron nodded with approval. "Great ass."

"I sort of thought so myself," Zack said.

"Better watch out for that kind, Zackie."

"Yeah?"

"You know what they call 'em, don't ya?"

Zack nodded. "I know, Byron."

Byron continued as though Zack hadn't spoken. "Back in Newport, Rhode Island, they call 'em the Fall River debs. In Pensacola, the Mobile debs. In Norfolk..."

"That what she was, Byron? A Norfolk deb?"

"Who?" Byron looked dumbly at his son, then he turned away as he caught Zack's drift. "Aw, shit, Zackie, let's not go off on your mother again. Please!"

"What if I want to talk about her, pard? What then?"

"Aw..."

"You know, that's all I've ever heard from you since I was a kid. You never want to talk about it."

"I don't!"

"Well, I do!"

"What the hell for?" Byron took a long pull on his beer.

"Because it's important, man."

"Well, I got nothin' to tell you. Two goddamn times I made it with your old lady. We barely even talked."

The jets roared by overhead, and Zack had to raise his voice to be heard.

"That's not how she told it. She said you wrote her every week you were away."

Byron waved his hand in dismissal. "I wrote, but not every week."

"She said you told her in every letter how much you loved her, how you wanted to marry her, have children with her."

"I never said any of that!" Byron pulled out a cigarette and fired it up.

"You're lyin', pard. I found the goddamn letters, and I read every one of 'em. Right after she did it."

Byron shook his head and stared at his shoe. After a moment he looked up at his son. "Okay, I wrote those things."

"You bet you did."

"And I had some big thoughts of getting together with your mom. But when she hit me with being pregnant, I saw who she was."

"Meaning?"

Byron looked around to make sure no one would hear him. "Meaning that I'd had quiff lay that shit on me before!"

Zack stared at his father for a moment, unable to believe what he'd heard. "What did you call her?"

"Aw, come on, pard."

"What'd you call her, you son of a bitch?" Zack jumped to his feet, ready to knock Byron out of the bleachers.

"Zack, I…"

"She loved you, you bastard!"

The four jets made another pass over the field, and their thundering engines served to keep Zack and Byron's argument private.

Byron made a helpless gesture toward his son.

Zack wrinkled his lip in disgust. "And she believed you when you said you loved her! She never gave up thinking you'd come back."

"It's over, kid," Byron said. "There ain't nothin' I can do about it now."

"You can at least respect her memory." Zack bent over and wagged his finger in Byron's face. "You ever talk about her like that again, I'll kill you!" He stared at his father until Byron lowered his eyes, then Zack turned and elbowed his way out of the crowd.

He was halfway to his motorcycle when he heard the running footsteps behind him.

"Zack, wait!" Paula yelled.

He kept on walking. After a moment she came up beside him.

"What's the matter, Zack?"

He shook his head. "Nothing, Paula. Go on back to the show."

"I've seen all that a hundred times," she said. "I want to be with you, and I'd like to meet your father."

"Why don't you just leave me alone!" he snapped.

She stopped and watched his back as he kept going toward his bike. "Yeah, I'll leave you alone," she said. "How about forever? That long enough for you?" She turned around and headed back toward the field.

Zack started his motorcycle, turned it around, and watched Paula for a moment. He hated himself for acting in his old way. But it doesn't have to go on forever, he thought. He drove the motorcycle up alongside her and flashed her an apologetic smile. She kept on walking. Finally, he motored around in front of her and blocked her path. She flashed him a furious look. "Hey," he said, "isn't it about time you had me over for Sunday dinner?"

She looked at him as if he were crazy.

"Come on," Zack said. "Invite me. All day the idea of a family Sunday dinner has been coming into my head. Since you're the only one I know around here with family..."

"Zack!"

"Yeah?" He smiled.

"I don't know if I want to do that."

Sid and Lynette walked up, Lynette looking a little green around the gills. "I don't feel so hot, Paula," she said. "You mind goin' back?"

Paula looked at Zack, then at Lynette. "Naw. Let's go."

Sid kissed Lynette and patted her rear end. "You gotta stop partying so hard."

Paula gave Zack a perfunctory kiss on the cheek. "Be seein' you around." She and Lynette started for the Falcon.

"What about that Sunday dinner?" Zack yelled. "When are you gonna let me know?"

Paula turned and gave him her most feisty look. "When I'm good and ready."

Zack stared at her until she got into the Falcon and drove off with Lynette. "Women," he said, waving at her.

Sid climbed on the motorcycle behind him. "What's the matter, Sweet Pea? Y'all have a little fuss?"

Zack kicked the bike into gear and headed back toward the barracks.

On the ferry the girls both bought cups of coffee and took them out on the fantail to watch Port Rainier recede into the background.

"You serious about having him over?" Lynette asked.

Paula shrugged. "I really haven't made up my mind yet."

"Pretty serious step."

"I don't want to hurt his feelings by not asking, but I'm not sure I want all of them gawkin' at him."

"I know the feeling."

"Damned if I do, damned if I don't."

"Amen." Lynette took a large gulp of coffee.

"But then he's really supposed to like me, right?"

Lynette nodded skeptically.

"So if he doesn't go for my family it shouldn't make any difference, right?"

"Right." Lynette gazed out to sea. "But it probably will."

"Crap," Paula said.

Both girls watched the water for half a minute.

"Paula?"

"Huh?"

"How far would you go to catch Zack?"

"What do you mean?"

"You know what I mean." Lynette gave her a hard look. "Would you let yourself get pregnant?"

"No way." Paula shook her head and took a drink of coffee. "Why? Would you?"

Lynette looked away. "I never used to think I'd do something like that, but now I'm not so sure."

"Oh, Lynette," Paula didn't want to hear this.

"Well, I don't know if nine weeks is long enough to get a guy to fall in love with you."

Paula shook her head. "That don't justify trying to trap a boy by getting pregnant. Nothing justifies that."

"I don't know."

"I can't believe you're even thinking like that, Lynette. I mean, it's really backward."

"Says you."

"Well?"

"Well, it's no more backward than the way these hotshot assholes treat us. Fuck us and forget us." Lynette spat over the railing. "I mean, don't you ever feel used, Paula? Don't you ever feel that if this is all you get for your trouble then the son of a bitch ought to be paying for it?"

"No." It was Puget deb mentality; worse, it was whore mentality. "I never feel like that," Paula said.

"Well, I sure do."

You can't afford to, Paula thought. Once you started thinking that way there was no stopping it, and pretty soon you would end up pregnant. Then either you'd get dumped or else force someone who hated you into a marriage that would never work no matter how glamorous the life was. No, Paula thought. If Zack fucked her and forgot her it was her own fault. She knew the rules of the game before she started it. And besides, she thought she was good enough to attract a man on her own. She didn't have to trap him.

"Hey." She elbowed Lynette.

"Yeah?"

"I am going to invite Zack over to dinner. Next Sunday."

Lynette shook her head in amazement. "You're something else."

"Yeah," Paula said. "I am."

She asked her mother and father that night. Her mother was thrilled—a little too much so, Paula thought—and although her father put up some resistance, he finally relented and agreed to have Zack in his home. Paula called him on Monday, and he agreed to come. Then she had all week to worry. She didn't even get to spend Saturday night with him because of some extra training for the candidates, and by noon Sunday, as she helped her mother in the kitchen, she was so nervous she was about to throw up. Esther was nervous too, but she was doing her best to keep up Paula's spirits. "You look really pretty," Esther said.

Paula felt like a high school sophomore about to go on her first date. "You sure?"

Esther nodded. "I'm sure everything'll go just fine."

"Mom, I don't want to be a fool." She was beginning to doubt that she had done the right thing by inviting Zack. "I like him a whole lot, but..."

"Honey, you can only be yourself." Esther chucked her under the chin. "If that isn't enough for him..."

"Wait!" Paula held up her hand to silence her mother, then listened to Zack's motorcycle pull up in front and stop. "Oh, Jesus! He's here."

Paula and Esther peered out the window as Zack got off the motorcycle, adjusted his uniform, and started up the sidewalk with a bouquet of flowers in his hand.

"He's very handsome," Esther whispered. She seemed like a young girl again herself.

Paula eyed her mother for a moment, shook her head, and left the kitchen.

Joe Pokrifki sat in a chair by the living room window, watching the handsome officer candidate come up the walk. He gave his daughter a sullen look.

"Please, Daddy," Paula appealed. "Be nice to him."

Joe just stared at her. She turned away when the doorbell rang.

"Hi," she said, stepping out on the stoop.

"Hi, there." Zack reached up and kissed her. "That okay?"

Paula nodded, then pointed to the flowers. "Are those for me?"

Zack shook his head. "Your mom."

"Oh." She stood there looking at him for a moment.

"We gonna go in?" he asked.

"In a minute." She said nothing more.

"Uh, is there a password or something?"

"How was last week?" she asked.

"Lovely, lovely."

"Any more D.O.R.'s?"

He shook his head. "Why don't we get it over with, Paula. Or is there a mad dog inside or something?"

She stepped aside and stretched out her arm to escort him in. To hell with it, she thought. There wasn't anything she could do now.

To hell with it is right, she thought two hours later, two of the most uncomfortable hours she had ever experienced. Her father was like a stone, her sisters were so busy ogling Zack and giggling that they barely touched their food, and her mother kept looking at Zack with the moony eyes of a schoolgirl, asking him endless questions about the families of the other candidates, apologizing for her cooking, and telling embarrassing stories about Paula's childhood. They were almost finished with dessert when she said, "Thanks again for the flowers, Zack."

He nodded, swallowing some apple pie. "My pleasure, Mrs. Pokrifki." He looked up at Joe, who was giving him a hostile stare.

"How many more weeks till you graduate, Zack?" Esther asked.

He held up three fingers. "Just three, ma'am."

"But the roughest part is just coming up, right?"

Paula was embarrassed that her mother would know so much about the program. The old deb syndrome, once again. For a moment she wished she lived in Iowa or some place away from any large body of water.

"I hear it's rough," Zack said. "But personally I think the worst part is over." He smiled at her, then at Joe, but Joe's hard expression did not change.

"Excuse me, sir," Zack said, "but why're you looking at me like that?"

"Looking at you?" Joe said.

"Oh, Zack," Esther said. "He doesn't mean anything by it. Do you, Joe?"

Joe stared at his wife for a moment. "I don't mean anything by it." He looked down at his food, then began staring at Zack all over again.

Zack looked away, finished what was left of his dessert in three bites, then leaned back and rubbed his stomach. "Great dinner, Mrs. Pokrifki."

She gave him a long smile, saying nothing.

"Really great," Zack said. "Absolutely the best meal I've had in a long, long time."

"Oh, yes," she said after a moment. "Thank you, Zack."

Paula pushed back her chair and stood up, grabbing Zack's arm. "Come on, Zack," she said. "Let's go for a walk." She didn't think she could stand being at the table for another minute.

As they cleared the front gate and started up

the sidewalk, Paula burst into tears. Zack put his arm around her, and she sobbed helplessly for a few moments.

"It's okay," he said.

"I'm so embarrassed," she spluttered. "I knew I shouldn't have brought you here."

"It's okay," he said again. "Really. It was a great free meal. It's too bad everyone was so uptight. I really felt sorry for you."

"I thought I was used to it." She took a handkerchief out of her purse, wiped her eyes, and blew her nose. "Shit," she said.

"Forget it."

"Yes, sir."

They walked along in silence for a while, then she said, "So after you graduate you go on to basic flight school, right?"

He nodded.

"Pensacola?"

"Uh-huh." He looked up at the sky. "Then if I get jets it's on to Beeville, Texas."

"Zack?"

"Huh?"

"Do you ever think about what it'd be like to have kids? You know, a family?" She didn't even know why she said that. She knew it must have sounded all wrong.

"No," he said. "Why? Is that what you want?"

"Someday." She watched the Harper kid pedaling up the sidewalk on his tricycle. "When I'm sure I can do a better job of it than my folks."

"That's smart."

"They weren't so hot. As you saw."

"Whose are?" Zack shrugged. "So what would you do differently?"

"For a start, I wouldn't marry a man I wasn't in love with."

Zack kicked a stone off the sidewalk into the grass. "Why'd your mom marry that guy if she didn't love him?"

"Because my real father wouldn't marry her."

He stopped and looked at her for a moment. "Your real father?"

What the hell, Paula thought. I've come this far, I might as well go all the way. No false impressions. Take me as I am or let me go. The lines didn't seem too comforting as she pulled the tattered photo out of her wallet. "Yeah," she said. "Him." She still thought he was a good-looking guy with his stylish little mustache. Of course, the uniform of a flight candidate didn't hurt.

Zack looked at the picture for a long moment, shaking his head. "Your real father was an officer candidate? Like me?"

Paula nodded. "Twenty-two years ago."

"Jesus Christ!" Zack said.

"What?"

"No wonder your old, uh, stepfather was looking at me like that. I don't blame him."

"That's probably why my mom was looking at you the way *she* did."

"Yeah." He seemed nervous and kept shaking his head as they walked along. At the top of the street he turned and started them back toward the house. Halfway there he looked at his watch. "I think I probably should be heading back to the base."

"So soon?" She guessed she had scared him. But she wasn't going to beg him to stay. Give him time to think it over. Make up his own mind.

He nodded. "We got a lot to do to get ready for this week."

"I hope it goes okay."

"Thanks." He gave her a little kiss and climbed on his motorcycle.

"Call me during the week if you get a chance."

"I'll try." He started the bike. "But this week we go into survival training, so I can't make any promises."

She smiled. "No one's asking you to."

"Well, thanks again for dinner."

"Any time, Sweet Pea."

"And thank your mom again for me, will you?"

"Sure." She stared at him for a moment, fighting the thought that this was the last time she would ever see him. "Zack, I hope you know that I didn't have to show you that picture."

"I know, Paula. See you."

His smile was almost reassuring. Paula stood on the sidewalk and watched him until he turned off the street and disappeared. Well, she'd done it, and now she would just have to wait and see what happened.

On a street not far from the barracks, Sid and Lynette were locked in a passionate embrace in the Falcon when Zack pulled up along-side. He slapped his palm on the roof of the car. "Okay, children! Time to break it up."

"Hey, hoss!" Sid yelled. "You just saved me from bein' raped." He gave Lynette another kiss and jumped out of the car.

"How was your dinner, Zack?" Lynette asked.

"Mighty fine." He gave her a smile. "Best chow I've had in a long time."

"How'd you like mom and pop?"

"Real nice folks."

"Pop's a little quiet, isn't he?"

Zack nodded. "Pop *is* a little quiet."

Sid climbed on the motorcycle behind Zack. "See you next weekend, honey."

Lynette blew him a kiss. "See you, Zack," she said.

He nodded before driving off.

He parked the bike beside the barracks, and Sid jumped off and let out a rebel yell.

"Jesus, man," Zack said. "What's that all about?"

"I am in *love,* Mayo."

"Huh?"

"I kid you not, cool breeze."

Zack just shook his head.

Sid took a deep breath and looked heaven-ward. "I tell you, man, we must've set a new indoor record today. You want to know how many times we did it?"

"I do *not,*" Zack said. He started toward the barracks.

"What's with you?" Sid caught up with him, and they started up the stairs.

"It's what's with you that's wrong," Zack said.

"Hey, I'm fine."

"You're dumb, man. And you better get smart."

"What the hell is that supposed to mean?"

"It means it's time to walk away." Zack strode into their room, tossed his hat on his bunk, and began unbuttoning his uniform.

"You gotta be kidding," Sid said.

"You remember what Foley said? His little warning?"

"Sure, but..."

"Well, Paula and Lynette are the girls he was talking about. They're out to marry us any damn way they can."

Sid shook his head. "I don't believe that," he said softly.

"Then you're nuts. Or horny."

"They're just having a good time. Same as us." Sid sat down on his bunk and stared at his hands.

"That's what they want you to think. But I saw where she lived, man."

"So?"

"So I saw what she's trying to get away from."

Sid waved his hand in dismissal. "Big deal."

"It is a big deal!" Zack squatted down and waved his finger in front of Sid's face. "Just take my word for it, pard. Break it off now."

Sid shook his head.

"Do it this week." He stared hard at his roommate until Sid looked away.

9

The rain reminded Zack of a monsoon in the Philippines. He wondered if Foley had been able to order it from heaven, just to make their survival training a little more fun. "Come on, Della Serra," Zack said. "Gimme the goddamn shelter-half!" Della Serra handed it to him, and Zack tried to lash it to another one that he had already tied to a tree.

"Lookin' good, Mayo-naise," Perryman said.

"Here." Casey fitted her shelter-half over the side, then spread it over the top, hooking it up with Sid's to make a little lean-to for the five of them.

"Summertime," Sid sang. "And the livin' is easy."

Zack looked at his watch. One in the goddamn morning. A shaft of lightning split the black sky, then the thunder rolled ominously in the distance.

"Who knows what evil lurks in the hearts of men?" Sid said.

"That Foley's one evil bastard," Perryman said.

"Lay off, Perryman," Zack said. "You'll be grateful for this when your plane goes down in the jungles of El Salvador."

"Yeah," Sid said. "And them big forty-foot snakes come crawlin' after your ass."

"Shut up!" Della Serra said.

"There ain't no snakes up here, are there?" Perryman asked.

Zack guffawed. "Check your survival manual, Sweet Pea."

"I don't know about you guys," Casey said, "but I'm starving."

"The weaker sex." Zack played his flashlight on the dirt, then reached out and grabbed a fat black bug. "Here you go, See-gar." He held out the bug. "Let's see if you got any balls."

She looked at the ugly little specimen and wrinkled her lips in disgust.

"Come on, See-gar," Sid said.

"You can do it, Casey." Della Serra patted her on the back.

Zack dangled the bug in front of her. "This here'll give you the strength to get over the obstacle course."

"You sure that kind's on the list?"

"It is, Casey," Perryman said. "Now, no more excuses."

"How about you?" she asked.

Perryman shook his head. "I ain't hungry."

"Ha!" She reached out, grabbed the bug, and popped it in her mouth.

"Let's hear it for the little lady." Zack clapped his hands, and the others joined it.

Casey swallowed the bug and blushed with pride. Then she plucked another one off the wall of the lean-to and held it out to Zack. "Now let's see who's got the balls, Mayo-naise."

Zack shook his head and looked around at his companions. "Don't look at me," Della Serra said.

Sid guffawed. "It's on you, hoss."

"Seeger," Zack said, "sometimes you don't give a man a chance."

She nodded. "Eat it, Mayo."

He saluted. "Yes, sir!" He put the bug in his mouth and chewed.

"Man," Perryman said, "your face looks like a prune."

Zack swallowed, then took a long swig from his canteen. "You can't fool mother nature," he said.

"Ain't she a bitch," Perryman said as the roof began to leak.

"Hey," Zack said, "if we get through all this without drowning, I'm buyin' everyone a beer at T.J.'s on Friday night."

"I'll drink to that," Casey said.

"In case you turkeys don't know about T.J.'s, that's where the pilots hang out."

"How about your deb, Mayo?" Perryman asked.

"A deb is a deb is a deb," Zack said. "You gonna be there, Sid?"

Sid shrugged. "Who knows, hoss? Lotta things could happen between now and then."

The roof gave way entirely, dumping water on all five of them.

It was Zack's expert map reading and compass work that got them out of the forest ahead of the other teams, so he felt particularly buoyant when he and Sid skipped out of the barracks that afternoon. They were going to meet Sid's parents at the Holiday Inn for an early dinner, then on to T.J.'s for a party. He felt relieved not to have to worry about Paula, although part of him kept wondering what she would be doing tonight. Well, that's probably the way it would be for a few weeks. But by then he'd be long gone, just like a turkey through the corn.

"Mayo!"

He turned in the company street and looked back to the door of the orderly room where the officer of the day was standing. He feared being put on guard or some other petty detail that would ruin his weekend. "Yes, sir."

"Phone call, Mayo. Girl named Paula."

He looked at Sid, then at the ground, then back at the O.D. "Would you mind telling her that I already split, sir?"

"My pleasure, Mayo."

Zack snapped off a salute. "Thank you, sir!" He put his arm around Sid, and they headed for his motorcycle.

From her place on the production line, Lynette watched Paula at the pay phone. Bunny

Myles, a thirty-year-old, faded, jaded deb if there ever was one, came up beside her. "You and Paula still seeing those flight candidates over to the base?"

Lynette sneered at Bunny. "What makes you think we wouldn't be?"

Bunny shrugged. "It's Friday afternoon, and I ain't heard too much about what you're doin' this weekend."

"Is that right?"

Bunny nodded.

"Well," Lynette said, "I'm taken care of just fine."

Bunny nodded toward the phone. "What about Paula?"

"Why don't you ask her?"

Bunny sighed with cynical wisdom. "They're all the same, you know it?"

"They're not all the same," Lynette said. If they were, she was going to end up just like Bunny.

"It usually happens around the time they complete that survival training. Then they start to think they can make it without you. Just a couple of weeks left, what the hell difference does it make?"

"Bunny!"

"Suddenly they stop callin'. Bastards think they own the goddamn world."

Lynette shook her head. "You're a real cheerful person, Bunny."

"Got reason to be, kid." Bunny tucked in her plaid shirt with a philosophical flourish. "You know what they say about us, don't you?"

"Don't tell me," Lynette said.

Bunny surveyed the room with its grinding machinery and hardworking women. "Old debs never die, they just go on working at National."

Paula hung up the phone and walked over to them, a sad expression on her face.

Bunny patted her on the back. "He hasn't called you by now, honey, he ain't gonna."

"Bunny!" Lynette said. "Just keep your mouth shut. You don't know so much."

"They said he wasn't there," Paula said.

"Shit," Bunny said. "May they all crash and burn."

The tears flooded into Paula's eyes, and she turned and hurried off toward the exit.

"Paula!" Lynette yelled. "What're you doing? You better get back here!" You didn't risk losing your job because of these guys, that much Lynette knew.

Esther Pokrifki watched from her position on the conveyor as her daughter fled the room, then shut off the machine and followed her, catching up with her in the parking lot. She grabbed her arm. "Paula, wait!"

Paula turned and faced her mother. Esther's hair was tied up in a bandana, and, for someone under forty, she looked incredibly old. She looked around the parking lot at the battered cars, then up at the factory's huge smokestacks, which belched a bilious steam into the sky.

"Where you going?" Esther asked.

"Please, Mama. I can't go into it. Just let me go."

160

Esther grabbed her daughter and pulled her close. "You're going to the base to look for Zack."

She said nothing.

"Don't do it, Paula. Please!"

Paula rested her head on her mother's chest and let the tears come for a moment. "I love him, for God's sake."

"I know you do. But..."

"I can't just let him run off!"

"Oh, Paula!"

"It ain't just because he's gonna be a pilot, Mama. I love him for himself. I don't care what he is."

"But how're you gonna stop him if he don't want to be stopped?" Esther had begun to cry herself. "He'll just run all the faster."

"I don't know," Paula said. "But I've got to stop him somehow. Maybe if he just sees me."

Esther became suddenly agitated. "No!" she screamed. "Please, honey. I can't let you do that."

She gripped Paula so hard that it hurt. "Let me go, Mama."

"Don't go, baby."

Paula pulled free.

"Please don't go." Esther's chest heaved with a great sob, then she hung her head on her chest.

Now Paula comforted her. "Why are you crying like that, Mama?"

"Because I know what you're feeling." Esther wiped her eyes with her hand. "Don't do anything, Paula. Just let him go. It's the best thing."

"It can't be the best thing."

"Don't trick him or try to trap him."

Paula gave her mother a hard look. "But I'd never do something like that. Never!"

"Yes, you would!"

The two women stared at each other for a moment. Paula shook her head and turned to go, but Esther grabbed her by the arms and held her.

"Listen to me, Paula. If you go there tonight, and you find him..." She stopped and bit her lip.

"Say it, Mama."

"And it's the only way to hold on, you'll say anything, baby. You will. And God help you after that."

Paula gradually wriggled out of her mother's grasp. "That's somebody else you're talkin' about, Mama. It isn't me. I know it, and I know myself."

"Oh, God, Paula!"

Paula backed away a few steps. "I'll see you later, Mama." She gave her a little wave, then turned and ran away.

Sid and Zack arrived at the Holiday Inn before Sid's parents, so they went to the bar and had a couple of beers. Nothing was said about the girls. Zack didn't want to hear Sid rhapsodize about Lynette, and he didn't want to get any pressure about seeing Paula. He was half afraid he might give in and call her. No way! Instead, they talked about the program, the future, how exciting it would be at flight school. The only major hurdle left in their training was the decompression chamber, but that was supposed to be more weird than rough. Otherwise, they just had their final exam in aerodynamics—Zack knew he would have no trouble passing now—and their proficiency test on the obstacle course. And, of course, just keeping up with the day-to-day bullshit. There was no escaping staying on your toes.

"So, hoss," Sid said. "What're you gonna do on your leave?" They would have two weeks plus five days' travel time before reporting to Pensacola.

"Hell, I don't know." Zack hadn't even thought about it. "How about you?"

"I'll go down home. Got a few things to attend to."

"Sounds good." Zack drained his beer.

"You ought to come with me," Sid said. "Show you some good times."

"I might do it."

"Listen. You gotta do it." Sid became suddenly excited. "Seriously. You could have a room to yourself and everything."

"That's nice." Zack felt genuinely touched. "It'd be on the way to Florida too."

"You could push that Triumph down there in three days."

"Easy," Zack said.

Sid punched him on the arm. "Enough said, then. It's settled."

"What the hell. I ain't never been in Oklahoma before."

"You won't regret it," Sid said.

* * *

Despite their soft Oklahoma drawls, Sid's parents were about the most uptight people that Zack had ever met. Joe Pokrifki was just pissed off at officer candidates, and there was no blaming him for that. But Tom and Betty Worley looked as if they'd been born with ramrods up their rear ends. Their stiff moral fiber was apparent in every word they said or gesture they made. Zack wondered how Sid had turned out so loose and easy. Maybe the parents had tightened up after their son had been killed in Nam. Zack guessed that could do it to you. Still, Zack didn't mind being treated to a meal, and the prime rib tasted so good that he had to keep reminding himself to slow down so he wouldn't be finished with everything before the Worleys had finish their salads. Once he got commissioned, he was going to find someone to teach him proper manners. Or maybe he'd read an etiquette book or something.

Sid was telling his folks about Casey Seeger, and he mentioned how much trouble she was having on the obstacle course.

"It's too bad," Tom Worley said. "That always was a tough course."

Sid pointed at Zack. "Zack's only a tenth of a second off the all-time record. He's bound to break it before we leave."

Mrs. Worley smiled with pearly white teeth. "That's wonderful, Zack."

He shrugged as though it were nothing. "Your son is the one reason I'm still in the program, Mrs. Worley. He's pulled me through every exam."

Tom Worley dabbed his lips with a napkin. "You boys are lucky you didn't go through the program when I did. They used to start the Dilbert Dunker twice as high as it is now. And it was outside too."

"Brrr," Sid said.

Zack swallowed another mouthful. "That's really interesting, sir."

Tom Worley nodded. "And you couldn't just quit like you can now. When I went through it, and when my oldest boy went through it, if you bilged out you were sent into the fleet as a swabby."

And ended up in a Filipino whorehouse, Zack thought. He hoped that Tom wouldn't get going on the war stories.

"Sid," his father said, "how come you haven't written Susan in over three weeks?"

Sid stopped his fork a few inches from his mouth. He glanced at Zack, then gave his father a guilty look. "Gee, Dad, we haven't got much time." He popped some meat into his mouth, chewed, and swallowed. "I haven't written you for two weeks."

Betty Worley touched Zack's arm. "Zack, is my son involved with a local girl?"

"No, ma'am." Zack shook his head.

"I know about these girls," Tom Worley said.

Probably not too well, Zack thought. He looked Tom Worley straight in the eye. "All he ever talks about is Susan, sir."

* * *

"Thanks a lot," Sid said as he and Zack headed for Trader Jon's, the legendary T.J.'s. "Thanks for covering for me."

"No sweat," Zack said.

"You really bailed my ass out."

"Just one thing?"

"Name it, hoss."

"Who the hell is Susan?"

Sid looked at him sheepishly. "Didn't I ever tell you about her?"

"You ain't told me nothin' except about Lynette's ta-tas, as you call them."

"They're something else too."

"Yeah," Zack said. "Now, who's Susan?"

"My girl back home. We're supposed to get married after I get my wings."

"Oh." Zack shrugged. "But otherwise she's nothin' special, right?"

"She was Tommy's girl. They were engaged to get married before he died."

"That's rough."

Sid nodded. "I guess I should've told you about her. I don't know why I didn't."

"It's good to keep some things private."

"It ain't that," Sid said. "Maybe I didn't want you to think I was a shit for makin' it with Lynette."

Zack laughed. "That'd be the day. Hey, I ain't your folks, pard."

"Yeah."

"So, do you love this, uh, Susan?"

"She's the sweetest person I've ever known," Sid said. "She loves kids. Works with handicapped kids every afternoon at the church. Everybody loves her."

Zack shook his head. "I didn't ask you all that, Sweet Pea. I asked you if *you* loved her."

They stopped in front of T.J.'s and waved to Casey as she went inside. "I don't think I'm gonna make this party," Sid said.

"Huh?"

Sid smiled. "I'm meeting Lynette at the motel."

"Couldn't cut her loose, could you?"

"Best head in fifty-two states, good buddy. I mean, after three days of survival training, how could I resist?"

Zack decided not to press it about Susan. But he still felt that Sid was all wrong about Lynette. "You should've done what I did. A clean break."

"She said Paula was all tore up about you not calling his week."

Zack felt suddenly bad; then a wave of desire for Paula washed over him. He studied his shoe for a moment, then muttered "Uh-uh" beneath his breath. He looked up and gave Sid a big grin. "There's women for you, pard. They tell you they're in it for the laughs, but it's always a fucking lie."

"You're a tough one," Sid said.

Zack let out a little whoop. "Look out, T.J.! I'm in the mood for some fun!" He shook Sid's hand. "Have a good time tonight."

"I will," Sid said. "You try stayin' sober."

"Don't count on it." Zack walked up the steps and into T.J.'s.

* * *

As he sat down with Seeger, Perryman, and Della Serra, Casey poured him a beer from the pitcher and slid the mug across the table. "Drink up, Mayo-naise," she said. "You've earned it."

"To survival." He held up the mug, then drank the contents in less than five seconds.

"You still taste that bug?" Casey asked.

"Best bug I ever had." He admired Casey for seeming so nonchalant. She still hadn't made it through the obstacle course, and he knew she must be scared to death of failing. "And you showed me the way, See-gar."

"Have another one, Zack." Della Serra filled him up again.

"Much obliged." He had guzzled half of it when he heard a familiar laugh, and he turned to see Paula sitting across the room with the flight instructor who had tried to cut in on them the first time they were dancing. "Son of a bitch!" he muttered, and turned back to his classmates.

"Isn't that your deb, Mayo?" Casey asked.

He shrugged, then finished the rest of his beer.

"That guy's a hotshot flight instructor," Della Serra said.

Well, she didn't waste much time, Zack thought. For a moment he felt less guilty; then he began to feel mad. He poured himself another beer, drank deeply—wondering what the hell it was he should be feeling. Maybe just glad when he finally left this goddamn place.

"Sid couldn't leave his alone, huh?" Perryman asked.

Zack nodded. "Weakness of the flesh. Get you every time." He took another drink. "I'm the more mental type myself. Y'all have probably noticed that."

"I was hip to that the first day," Perryman said.

"That's why he never came on to me," Casey said.

"I was leavin' you for Foley, See-gar."

They all laughed. Zack looked over his shoulder and saw Paula standing nonchalantly at the jukebox. He watched her punch a couple of selections, then he stood up and walked over to her. A genuine surprise registered on her face when she saw him.

"Hi," he said.

"Zack!" She looked at him for a moment. "What're you doing here?"

"Just suckin' some suds with my classmates. We were all on survival together. With Sid."

"Oh."

"Anyway, I had to see the legendary T.J.'s once before I left this place."

"Quite a spot," she said.

"You come here a lot?" His stomach was finally settling down.

"Once in a while." She seemed unenthused.

Zack looked over at the flight instructor, then back at her. "I know I should've called you, but you couldn't believe the week we had."

"That's okay." There was no sign at all of

hostility on her face. "How'd it go in survival training?"

"Okay, I guess. We survived."

"It looks like it."

"How'd your week go?" He felt like a tenth grader.

"Same old thing." She shrugged. "I'm getting a fifteen-cent raise at the beginning of the month."

"That's great." His smile felt pasted on his face.

She nodded. After a moment, she said, "Well, a couple more weeks and you'll graduate."

"Yeah. It's starting to feel like I might make it."

"See, I told you. All you had to do was see it that way and it happened."

"Yeah." He remembered the touch of her arms the first time he danced with her. "You told me." He fought a desire to bend down and kiss her. He was staring at her intensely, and after a few seconds she looked away.

"Well," she said, "I better get back to my date." She started to turn away, but he grabbed her hand.

"Paula?"

"Yeah?" Her eyes were incredibly green.

"I wanted to say something." He was fumbling for words.

"Yes, Zack," she said calmly.

"I mean, I just wanted to say, uh, thanks."

She looked at him questioningly, unwilling to make it easier for him.

He looked at the jukebox, then back at her.

"I don't know how I'd have gotten through all that crap without, uh, you know, something to look forward to."

She smiled, in perfect control. "Don't thank me for nothing. I had a great time."

"I'm glad," he said feebly.

"Good luck in flight school." She reached up and grabbed his arm at the biceps. "I hope you get jets." She gave his arm a squeeze, then let it go and walked back to her date.

He watched her until she sat down, then, for fear that he was going to start talking to himself, he headed for the bar. He got a bottle of tequila and four small glasses and walked over to his classmates. He gave them a silly grin. "Hi, guys. I'm gonna teach you a little game I picked up in the Philippines. It's called 'one on one.' I drink one, then you drink one." He filled the glasses, put one each in front of Seeger, Perryman, and Della Serra, then picked up his and downed it in a gulp.

The others just sat there watching him.

"Come on, you guys. It's your turn."

"Hey," Perryman said. "I gotta go see my wife in a little bit. Can't be too screwed up."

"Aw!" Zack filled another glass and tossed it off.

"Hey, Zack," Casey said. "Why not take it easy?"

"I never could drink that stuff straight," Della Serra said.

"Oh, man." Zack looked at them all with disgust. He looked over his shoulder and saw Paula staring at him. He quickly turned away, filled another glass, and drank it. Then he pulled out his wallet and threw a wad of bills on the table. "C'mon, dick-brains! Fifty bucks says I drink all three of you under the table."

The last thing he remembered was Perryman pulling and Casey and Della Serra pushing him into a cab. He let out an insane laugh, then tried to pull Casey in with him. "C'mon, Seegar!" he bellowed. "Let's you and me go to the Tides Inn Motel." He pulled her down on top of him and kissed her.

She pushed back and escaped his grasp. "You're cute, Mayo," she said. "But you don't want me."

"I do, I do!" he yelled.

"And to tell you the truth, I don't want you."

"Heartless," Zack said.

"See you back at the base," she said.

"I'll make sure he gets in bed," Perryman said.

As the cab drove off, Zack thought he might call Byron when he got to the barracks, maybe go on a little toot with him, but the next thing he knew it was noon on Saturday, and he was waking up in his bunk with one prodigious hangover.

10

Sid was just about to doze off when he felt Lynette stir beside him. She pulled back the covers and quietly got out of bed. "Hey," Sid said.

"What?"

"Where you goin'?"

She slid into her panties and hooked on her bra. "It's eleven-thirty. I've got to catch the ferry."

"Oh, man," Sid groaned.

"I'm sorry, honey."

"Why don't you just spend the night. What are they gonna do, cut your allowance?"

"They might throw me out of the house. I can't risk that just now. My old lady's really been on the rag lately."

Sid watched her button up her blouse. "Speaking of that," he said, "isn't it about time you had a period?"

"I guess."

"Well?"

She pulled on her jeans. "I'm a little late, that's all." She shrugged as though it were nothing.

Sid sat up in bed. "How late?"

She sat down beside him and began putting on her shoes. "What difference does it make?"

"It'd make a lot of difference."

She patted him on the cheek. "If anything was to happen, which I'm sure it isn't, it would be my responsibility."

"Exactly how late are you, Lynette?" He tried to shake off his panic, but he had begun to feel very cold inside.

"What do you care?" She stood up and gave him a coquettish smile.

"How can you say that?"

"Suppose I was pregnant. Just suppose it."

It was a prospect he did not face with equanimity. "Yeah?"

"You don't think I'd try to make you do anything you don't want to, do you?"

He held out his hand to stop her. "Hold it, Lynette. You're way off base."

"Huh?" She looked at him uncomprehendingly.

"Your forcing me to do something isn't the only issue here. There's a lot more to it than that."

She shook her head as though she didn't understand. "What other issue is there, Sid?"

"My responsibility." He swung his legs over the side of the bed and pulled on his drawers.

He felt ridiculous talking this way in the nude. "My responsibility as its father."

"Oh, Sid..."

"I mean, if I've made you pregnant, I'd, uh, want to do the right thing." His mind was working fast, trying to figure out what the right thing was. Don't panic, man, he told himself. All problems can be solved.

"Yeah?" Lynette looked at him expectantly.

"I mean, I'd want to pay for the abortion."

She stared at him, saying nothing.

"I'd want to be with you through the whole thing. By your side."

"Oh." She grabbed her sweater off the chair and put it on.

"So how late are you, Lynette?"

"Never mind," she said coldly. "Let's just wait and see what happens."

"But..."

"Besides, I'm late for the goddamn ferry." She walked over to the bed and gave him a little kiss.

"See you tomorrow," he said.

"Yeah." She opened the door.

"And don't worry. Everything'll work out for the best."

"Sure thing." She stepped into the night and slammed the door.

He sat on the edge of the bed, first listening to the surf, then to the sound of Lynette's Falcon as it started up and drove off. Jesus Christ, he thought. Some pickle you got yourself into this time, hoss. He briefly regretted not following Zack's advice, but he knew he and Zack were entirely different people. And he *did* like Lynette. A lot. He had had more fun with her than he ever did with Susan. God, poor Susan. How would she feel if she ever found out? It was too damn easy to hurt people's feelings or get hurt yourself. He lay back down and rested his arm on his forehead. Would he be wrong to insist on an abortion? The poor girl was Catholic, so having one would probably be some kind of mortal sin for her, something she'd feel guilty about all her life. It wouldn't be right to put her through that. But he wasn't ready to start being a father, and he was sure Lynette wasn't ready for motherhood. It wouldn't be right to put the kid through that, and it wouldn't be any picnic for him. A great situation, he thought. No matter how you look at it, everybody loses. He got up and turned on the television, but there was nothing to take his mind off his worries. He went out and walked on the beach for an hour, returning to his room more confused than when he had gone out. The classic no-win situation. He consoled himself with several beers and several clichés, the last one of which was that he had put the cart before the horse. He fell asleep thinking that the only real choice he had was to wait until he had some concrete news. The consolation was not overwhelming.

"This is it, worms!" Foley bellowed from the hallway. "You got five minutes to get in your sweats and fall out in the company street. Now move!"

Zack had barely gotten out of his fatigues

when Sid tore out of the room like a whirlwind, his shoes in his hand.

"What the hell's with him?" Perryman said. "He's been like a zombie all week."

Zack shook his head. "Woman trouble, I reckon."

"The worst kind," Perryman said.

"Yeah, and he ain't even talkin' about his. I mean, I figure it must be woman trouble."

Perryman nodded. "You don't think his deb..."

"Don't even say it," Zack said.

"I heard that."

"Good luck on the O. course."

"You too," Perryman said. "You feel up for that record today?"

"This is the last shot." Zack pulled on his sweatpants, bent over, and touched his palms on the floor. "It'd be nice."

"I hope you do it, man. Leave our class on the map."

"Let's go," Zack said.

They ran down the stairs, and at the bottom Zack saw Sid huddled against the pay phone, his face the very picture of earnestness. "Come on!" Zack motioned for Sid to come.

Sid waved him away and went on talking.

"Oh, man." Zack shook his head at Sid, then went out to the formation. Sid joined them two seconds before Foley called the group to attention, and Zack didn't even have time to ask him what the hell was going on. As if it wasn't clear enough at this point. Goddamn Lynette, Zack thought. Goddamn debs, period. As they marched toward the obstacle course, he tried to clear his mind of all this garbage. He'd been thinking about Paula and had almost called her a couple of times, and now his roommate was so screwed up about this broad that he could hardly talk. No good, Zack thought. Especially with graduation so close. Blow it out! He took a deep breath and exhaled. Forget it all. Just get your commission and get the hell out of this place.

Sid was one of the first to go on the obstacle course, and once he had started, Zack quit worrying about him and began to focus on going after the record. His adrenaline was building higher and higher. Della Serra started, and Casey stepped up to the line. Zack studied Foley; he knew the D.I. wanted Casey to get over the wall, but it was something he couldn't show.

"Go get 'em, See-gar!" Zack said.

She turned and gave him a nervous thumbs up.

After Della Serra had cleared the inner tubes, Foley turned and gave Casey a hard look. "Ready, Seeger?"

"Yes, sir." She didn't even look at him.

"Go!" Foley bellowed, and Casey took off like a little rabbit.

Perryman went next, and Zack stepped up to the line. He closed his eyes and took a deep breath, shaking his arms loose at his sides.

Foley turned and looked at him. "I'm glad I gave you some extra training on this, Mayonaise."

"Yes, sir."

"Don't think you'd've made it otherwise."

"Yes, sir." Zack grinned, looking straight ahead.

"You ready, Mayo?"

"Yes, sir."

Foley looked down the course, then back at him. "Go!"

Zack was gone. Like a bat out of hell. Things seemed suddenly to get quieter as he sprinted the first fifty yards; then, as he began dancing through the inner tubes, he heard the first cries of his classmates cheering him on, and the music was the sweetest that he could remember. He went hand-over-hand through the horizontal ladder, then churned through the ankle-deep sand, concentrating hard on not slipping. He went over the low hurdles, his shorts barely skimming the bars, ran another twenty-five yards, and hit the dirt. He rolled on his back, dug his heels and elbows into the ground, and pulled himself under the low horizontal bars. It had never gone this well. He knew he was at least two or three seconds faster than he had ever been before. He passed Perryman on another short run, his roommate yelling "Go, Zack!" as he went by. He went up the angled beam as though he were a squirrel, jumped the moat without getting his feet wet, then lowered his head and sprinted full tilt toward the ten-foot wall.

When he raised his head, he could see Casey struggling up the rope. "Come on, Seeger!" he yelled. He jumped, caught the other rope, and started to climb. "Let's go over it together." He passed her, pivoted on the top of the wall, and was about to drop to the ground on the other side when he saw her fall back. Then everything seemed to come to a stop. He looked out from his perch and saw Foley in the distance, watching them. He studied his classmates as they poured their hearts into the exercises, and he was suddenly overwhelmed with feelings that he did not understand. "Hell with it," Zack muttered. He pivoted again and dropped into the sand beside Seeger.

"Go on, Zack!" she said, the tears starting out of her eyes. "Go for the record!"

He shook his head. "Fuck the record."

"But..."

"Now you listen to me and do exactly as I tell you."

She nodded helplessly as he drew a line in the dirt with his foot.

He pointed back a little way. "Now you start back ten yards and take off from here. Not there, or there," he said, pointing to two other spots, "but here."

"I don't..."

"No excuses, Seeger! You are going to plant those legs here, and then you *will* haul your pretty little booty over that wall. Because you have to. You want jets?"

She nodded.

"Then do it, goddamnit!"

"Yes, sir!" she said, and there was nothing funny about it.

They started together, caught the ropes and began the slow ascent, hand-over-hand. Twice she groaned, and twice Zack growled, "Do it!"

He made the last pull ahead of her; then he sat on the wall and looked down at her beet-red face. She looked as if she was about to let go. "One more!" he whispered sharply.

She took another breath, brought her right hand up over her left and struggled to the top of the wall. She gave Zack an exhausted smile, then the two of them pivoted together and dropped to the sand below. She almost beat him over the last fifty yards.

As they crossed the finish line, he reached out and cupped one of her buttocks in his hand. "I knew you had it in there, See-gar."

She let his hand linger for a few seconds before slapping it away. Then she turned and hugged him. "Thank you, Mayo-naise," she said.

"Always glad to be of service to the weaker sex." He scampered away before she could hit him and was in the middle of a laugh when he turned and saw Sid standing off to the side, gazing into space. Zack stopped laughing and shook his head. "Jesus Christ," he muttered. "Hey, Sid!"

The big Okie turned and looked at him, saying nothing.

Zack put his arm around Casey. "Guess who just finished the obstacle course?"

Sid looked at Casey and smiled softly. "Hey, Casey, that's great," he said without much enthusiasm. "Sorry I missed it. You get the record, Zack?"

"Naw." Zack shook his head.

"Too bad." Sid turned away and looked out at the hills.

Zack patted Casey on the back, then nodded toward Sid. "Me and this boy got some talking to do."

It took until dinnertime before Zack got his chance. Although Foley seemed pleased with the class's performance on the obstacle course—he even gave Seeger grudging compliments—he kept at them all afternoon with rifle drills, another hour of martial arts instruction, and a preparatory lecture on the decompression chamber. They had a few minutes in their room before chow, but every time Zack asked Sid what was wrong, "Nothing, hoss" was all he heard.

After a while Perryman left them alone, and Zack finally turned on his roommate. "Come on, man," he said. "What the fuck is it?"

Sid looked up at him, shocked.

"Jesus!" Zack said. "You've been walkin' around with your head in the clouds. You're not the Sid I know anymore. Now what is it?"

Sid stared at him for a moment, then spread his hands in defeat. "She's pregnant, hoss."

"She's..."

"Don't say 'I told you so.'"

Zack shook his head. "I won't."

"Thanks."

"You sure?"

"Yeah." Sid squeezed his cheeks between his hands.

"So what's the deal?"

"I reckon I'm gonna marry her."

"Marry her?"

"You heard me." Sid forced a smile. "I like her well enough. I think I'm even in love with her."

Zack let that one go by. They were called down to chow, and as they descended the stairs Zack brought up the possibility of an abortion.

"She won't hear of it," Sid said.

"Oh, man." Zack shook his head. "Selfish bitch," he muttered.

Sid said nothing, and the two of them remained silent until they were halfway through the chow line. "It's a big religious thing with her," Sid said. "She don't even want to discuss it."

"But of course she wants you to marry her."

Sid shrugged. "She said it was up to me. She said if I don't, she'll go off somewhere by herself and have the baby."

Zack noticed a couple of the other candidates pricking up their ears.

"Sort of puts me between a rock and a hard place," Sid said. "If you get my drift."

"I got it," Zack mumbled.

"So what do I do?"

"If she wants to have it so bad, let her go have it. Girls do that all the time. It ain't no big problem."

"I can't do that." Sid shook his head. "I can't just sit by and not do anything."

"I don't see why not." If Lynette had been there, Zack felt he would have punched her in the face.

"If it's my kid too, then I've got a responsibility. Don't I?"

"Uh-uh, buddy. Not if she won't even talk about an abortion."

"You don't get it, do you?"

"Get what?" Zack said. "I get the fact that you're gettin' the shaft."

"But it would still be my kid. That's the point."

Zack gave him as cold a look as he could muster. "Do you know that for sure?"

Sid eyed him for a moment. "It's mine."

Zack thought of inventing some story that Paula had told him Lynette was screwing other guys, but he didn't have the heart for it. "Okay," he said. "But what if it's the way Foley told it? What if she just got knocked up to trap you?"

"Yeah?"

"Is it still your responsibility?"

"I guess it don't matter anymore," Sid said. "I mean, no matter how it happened, if she goes ahead and has it, there'll be a child in the world that's mine. I don't know. I just couldn't go through life knowing that and not knowing it's name or where it lived."

"Jesus Christ, Sid! Is everything your responsibility?"

Sid gave him a hard look as they sat down, but Zack couldn't let up.

"Look at your life, man. Your brother gets killed instead of you. Isn't that why you promised to marry this Susan?"

Sid looked at him briefly, then took a forkful of salad.

"Isn't that why you do everything, man?" Zack taunted. "Out of some bullshit code of ethics you inherited from your family?"

Sid slapped the table with his hand. "Maybe it's all bullshit to you!" he yelled. "But that's not the way I was raised. I believe we have a responsibility to the people in our lives, that that's the only thing that separates us from the goddamn animals!"

"Aw." Zack looked around to see several of the others watching them.

"I'm not like you, Mayo," Sid said. "I can't just shit on people and then sleep like a baby all night."

Zack toyed with the pork chop on his tray, then looked back at Sid. "You got a responsibility to yourself first, pard."

"I figured that's what you'd say."

"Well, if you can't handle that fact, then you've got bigger problems than getting some girl pregnant!"

They both stared at each other; then Foley walked up to the table and tapped it with his swagger stick. "I believe we're here to eat, gentlemen."

"Yes, sir," Sid said.

"You hear me, Mayo?" Foley said.

"Yes, sir!" Zack cut into his pork chop viciously.

They didn't talk about it anymore. After chow they went back to their room for the regular evening ritual of polishing boots and brass, squaring away their other gear, studying aerodynamics, and trying to get some sleep. Sid drifted off into his own world once again, and Zack joked with Perryman about the program and how they would fare in flight school. He kept trying to think of something to say to Sid that would really knock him on his ass, something to make him convince Lynette to have an abortion. Failing that, he had to force him to give up this marriage idea—let her have the baby on her own if it was such a big deal. No wonder the world was such a screwed-up place.

The thought of people and their follies made his flesh crawl, and later, as he was brushing his teeth, he began to fall into a profound depression. At first he thought it was just because of Sid, but as he lay in bed and tried to sort it out, he began to think about his mother and Byron, and, naturally, himself. He wondered if Byron had tried to talk his mother into an abortion. They had both been Catholic—albeit lapsed—and abortions weren't that easy to come by back in those days (although he guessed that around Norfolk there must have been someone who took care of those things). He wondered if his mother had tricked Byron to get him to marry her, and at last he visualized Byron sitting in a bar with one of his swabby buddies, Byron contemplating marriage while the swabby urged him to cut out. Well, whatever the situation was, his mother had gotten pregnant, and Byron had cut out, and Zack had been born to grow up without a father. And now here he was urging his friend to do the same thing.

"Jesus!" he muttered, momentarily furious at all the dead-end situations that life so generously presented. He heard Sid moan, and looked over to see him curled up in the fetal position, his face to the wall. Maybe the situation was more complicated than Zack had thought. Maybe Sid was even doing the right thing, or at least the best thing for the kid under the circumstances. At least the child wouldn't have to grow up with no father in a nowhere place and be another jerk with no sense of himself. Fucking Byron, Zack thought, wondering how many of his other children were stumbling around Mobile or Hong Kong or San Diego or wherever. He guessed that maybe Sid's sense of responsibility wasn't such a bad thing after all, even if it did get wasted on Lynette. In any case, Zack wasn't going to bug him anymore. If Sid wanted to talk, he could initiate it himself, and Zack would be glad to listen and offer whatever advice he could. Otherwise, the best thing he could do was to try to keep up Sid's spirits and let him know he had a friend no matter what.

The decompression chamber wasn't much bigger than a closet. Sid and Zack sat at one small table, Perryman and Seeger at another, and Della Serra and Warde at another. They all wore oxygen masks, and they all were playing pat-a-cake while Foley and an instructor watched from behind a thick window. This was the way to finish up the program, Zack thought. Slapping hands like a bunch of two-year-olds.

"Okay, candidates," the instructor said over the intercom. "I want everyone to take off their masks and continue the same exercise."

The candidates did as they were told.

"The purpose," the instructor continued, "is to show you the effects of altitude on the motor skills when you've been cut off from your oxygen."

Zack and Sid smiled at each other as a whining sound was added to their new sensations. Zack slapped Sid's hands, then clapped his own, then slapped Sid's once again. He could already feel some deterioration in his reactions, but he kept reminding himself not to panic or to try to do more than he could. He breathed as regularly as possible, but he was beginning to feel light-headed and a bit silly.

The whining grew louder, and Sid and Zack kept missing each other's hands. Zack had trouble clapping his own hands, but he went at it deliberately, not looking at Sid until he had accomplished his task.

He glanced up with a smile, ready for another round of pat-a-cake. Sid was staring at his own hands, trying to get them to clap, but missing every time. Zack had never seen so much fear and panic on his face. "Sid!" he said.

Sid's eyes met his, but it was as though Sid didn't know him. "Stop this thing!" Sid yelled.

"Just relax!" Zack said, holding up his hands.

"I said *stop it!*" Sid looked crazily around the room, then put his hands on the table and pushed himself into a standing position.

"Sit down, man!" Zack said. "I'll get you through this. If you panic, you're done."

Sid didn't hear him. He lurched like a drunk toward the door of the chamber, then stopped and gave everyone a horrified look. He covered his ears with his hands, took one more step, and tripped. "I want out!" he yelled as he hit the floor.

Zack tried to get up, but his reactions were so slow that he felt like a sloth moving down a branch. "Sid!"

"Let me out!" Sid screamed. "Please!" He rolled on his side and began to cry.

Zack weaved across the room and dropped to his knees by Sid's side. "It's okay, Sid."

"Let me out!"

"Try not to be afraid," Zack said. "Talk to yourself, man. Talk yourself out of it."

The whining stopped, and they began to back off on the pressure inside the chamber.

"Let me out," Sid sobbed. "I just want to get out of here."

Zack cradled Sid in his arms for a moment. As he began to feel more normal, he said, "What happened, Sid?"

Sid stretched out and shook as though he were terribly cold. "I don't know, Zack. I just don't know. I felt like, uh, like I was suffocating." He put his hand to his face and sobbed again. "Christ, man, I was so scared. I've never been so goddamn scared."

Zack wiped the tears off Sid's face. "You gotta stop crying, man."

"I can't."

"Do it!" Zack said sternly. "You can't let the instructors see it." But he knew it was already too late. He glanced around at his classmates, who were all staring solemnly at Sid. Then the door to the chamber opened and a grim-faced Foley stepped in, the instructor behind him.

Zack and Sid didn't get a chance to talk about it. Sid was gone for half the evening, and when he slumped back into the room around nine o'clock, he told Zack he wanted to be left alone. Sid polished his boots and his brass in silence, then crawled into his rack and seemed to go to sleep. At least he must still be in the program, Zack thought. Wouldn't be doing all this stuff otherwise.

Zack had to leave early in the morning for colors duty—helping to raise the flag—and he went straight from the flagpole to the mess hall where he found Perryman, but no Sid. "Where's he at?" he asked his other roommate.

Perryman shrugged. "Beats me. I had latrine duty. He wasn't in the room when I got back."

"I hope he's all right," Zack said.

"You and I both know he ain't."

Zack nodded. "You know what I mean."

"I reckon I do," Perryman said.

Zack finished his chow and hurried back toward the barracks. He happened to glance up at the orderly room as he went by, and he suddenly stopped in his tracks. Foley and Sid were coming down the steps, Sid dressed in his civvies. As they got to the bottom of the steps, Zack looked at Sid, whose face was like stone, and then to Foley. "You didn't kick him out?"

Foley and Sid continued walking.

Zack watched them for a moment, then caught up. "Wait, sir!" he said to Foley. "Didn't he tell you what he's been going through?"

"It don't matter what he's going through." Foley kept his eyes straight ahead. "That's the whole purpose of this zoo, Mayo."

"Huh?" Zack said.

"What matters is that he freaked out for *some* reason at twenty-five thousand feet. That can't happen again."

"But you don't understand," Zack pleaded. He looked to Sid for support, but Sid seemed as determined as Foley. What the hell was going on? Zack touched Foley's arm. "There's this girl he's gotten pregnant, and she's putting him through hell, sir."

Sid turned and gave him a sharp look. "He's right, Zack. It doesn't matter."

Zack shook his head and held out his arms, dumbfounded. "Just like that? It's all over?"

Sid nodded.

"With less than two weeks to go, you're out?"

Foley turned and stared at him. "It can still happen to you too, Mayo." He marched off like a windup toy.

Zack felt a sudden stab of fury. "Come back here, motherfucker!" he screamed, too mad even to regret it.

Foley whirled, his eyes gleaming. "What'd you call me, Mayo? Did I hear you right?"

"Zack!" Sid said. "Don't!"

Zack looked at Sid, then back at Foley. "I thought the D.I.'s were supposed to help you in this place! What the hell kind of human being are you?"

"Stop eyeballing me, Mayo, or you're out!"

For a moment Zack felt surprised that Foley hadn't kicked him out already.

"Please, Zack!" Sid yelled. "Just leave it alone. Go back to the barracks."

Zack didn't even look at him. "I don't get it," he said to Foley. "He's the best candidate in our class. Ask anyone. The best student, the best leader, the best friend to everybody! Doesn't that count for something? I mean, couldn't you bend your goddamn standards just a little!"

Foley pointed at him and opened his mouth.

"Zack!" Sid said. "It wasn't him!"

Zack looked from Foley to his roommate.

Sid nodded slowly. "He didn't even ask me to D.O.R. I came to him on my own."

Zack looked back at Foley. The D.I. stood at rigid attention, ever the dutiful soldier.

Sid touched him on the shoulder. "I'm glad it's over, Zack. I really mean that."

"I don't think you know what you're doin'," Zack said. "I think that broad's got your head turned all around."

"I don't belong here," Sid said. "It's just like everything else in my life. I wasn't doin' it for me. Hell, I don't want to fly jets. Or I want to fly 'em for my dad and brother." The tears suddenly welled up in Sid's eyes, and his jaw began to shake. He looked mournfully at Zack for a moment, then turned and ran between the buildings as fast as he could go.

"Sid, wait!" Zack screamed. "Where the hell you going?"

Sid kept on running, not looking back.

Zack started after him, then turned and faced Foley. He came to attention and saluted the D.I. "With your permission, sir!" he said.

Foley returned the salute and nodded once.

Zack ran to the barracks, but Sid wasn't there. He looked in a few other places on the base, but no Sid. He must have caught a cab or an early bus and gone to see Lynette. What was the dumb bastard going to do? Sit around the factory and talk to her on her coffee breaks? Zack ran back to the barracks again, changed into his dress uniform—they wouldn't let him off the base in fatigues—then hopped on his Triumph and headed for Port Angeles.

He weaved in and out of traffic on his way to the ferry, furious at Sid for quitting, furious at Foley for letting him, and furious at Lynette for provoking the whole damn thing. What a goddamn mess! It wasn't until Zack was actually on the ferry and could do nothing about getting to Port Angeles any faster that he began to think about himself. He had almost gotten his ass thrown out this morning. He drank some coffee and shook his head. Wouldn't that have been something. Maybe Sid would have gotten back in the program, and maybe Lynette's period would have come, and there would be old Zack, thrown out for calling Foley a motherfucker. Keep cool, man, Zack told himself. There were still a couple of weeks to go. He experienced a moment of gratitude for Foley's overlooking his indiscretion—the son of a bitch *could* bend the rules—but then the ferry docked at Port Angeles, and Zack sped off toward the looming smokestacks of the National Paper Company.

Lynette had the day off. So did Paula and Paula's mother. It made Zack even more pissed off to have wasted the time coming to the factory, and the way the other women looked at him made him downright sullen. Deb heaven, he thought, as he sped away. Would he be glad when he left for Florida!

Esther Pokrifki was working in the garden when Zack pulled up. "Hi, Zack," she said, standing up. "How are..."

"Is Paula here?" he asked coldly.

The front door opened, and Paula came out in her jeans and a flannel shirt. "Hi, Zack." She started down the walk.

He looked at her for a moment, then glanced away. "I'm lookin' for Sid."

She stopped by the front gate. "So?"

"So he D.O.R.'d, and I don't know where the hell he is."

Paula shrugged. "Why'd he do that?"

Zack turned and faced her, shaking his head with disgust. "You know goddamn well what happened."

"I do?"

"Let's not play games, Paula. I need to find him."

"I'm not playing any games!" she yelled. "Go look at Lynette's. That's the logical place."

"I don't know where that is."

Paula opened the gate, walked out to the motorcycle, and climbed on the back. "Turn around." She waved to her dumbfounded mother as they sped down the street.

Lynette was sitting doing her nails on the steps outside her house—the same house she had lived in all her life—when the cab pulled up. The back door opened, and Sid jumped out, dressed in civvies, and with a lunatic grin on his face.

"What the...?" Lynette trailed off, unable to finish.

"Hi, babe." Sid gestured for her to come over by the Falcon.

"Hi." She watched the cab drive off.

"Come on," Sid said. "I've got a couple of things I want to tell you."

All of a sudden it hit her. This was a weekday. He wasn't supposed to be here. "What're you doing out of uniform, Sid?"

"Aw."

"You don't want to get in trouble."

"Forget that." Again he gestured toward the Falcon. "I got a little surprise."

She pointed to the curlers in her hair. "I can't go like this."

"You're beautiful."

"Can't you wait a few minutes till I'm ready?"

"No way," he said, but he walked over to the

porch and kissed her anyway. "I'm so happy I'm about to bust."

"You sure look it."

"Here, honey." He reached in his pocket and drew out a little box. "This is for you." He handed it to her. "It cost me my whole savings, but I said what the fuck."

She opened the box and found herself staring at a diamond engagement ring. "Sid! It's beautiful!" She looked up at him with a big smile spread across her face. "You mean...?"

"That's right." He nodded. "Let's get married, Lynette. Let's find a justice of the peace and just do it."

She tried on the ring and it fit perfectly. She stood up and took a deep breath, nearly overwhelmed by her sudden euphoria. She turned and looked at her ramshackle house, thrilled that soon she would be out of it forever. "Oh, Sid! Let's go tell Paula!"

He smiled up at her.

"God!" she screamed. "I wonder where we'll be stationed first. I hope it'll be Hawaii. I've always wanted to go to Hawaii."

Sid reached up and grabbed her arm. "We're not gonna be stationed anywhere, baby."

"Huh?"

He nodded. "I D.O.R.'d."

She felt as if someone had slapped her in the face. Or maybe hit her on the jaw. She felt suddenly loose inside, as though all her muscles were melting. "You D.O.R.'d?"

"I had to."

"But why? You didn't. Not really."

"I'm no aviator, baby. I was faking it, like I was with everything else in my life. Up until right now, that is."

Lynette shook her head and looked down at the steps, almost expecting to find the pieces of her dream at her feet. "But where would we go?"

"Oklahoma," he said proudly.

"And do what?"

He shrugged as though there were no problem. "I can get my old job back at J.C. Penney's. In a couple of years I'll be floor manager."

"Sounds great." She couldn't bear to look at him.

"You'll love Oklahoma, Lynette. You and mama'll get along just great. Money'll probably be a little tight for a while, but we'll make it. Who knows, maybe in a couple of years I'll go back to college. Become a lawyer or..."

"Sid!"

"What, honey?"

"There ain't no baby, Sid."

He gave a little twitch with his head and blinked. "Come again?"

"I'm not pregnant. I got my period this morning."

He just stared at her, saying nothing.

"There's no baby, Sid!" She said it as though it were his fault.

"Well," he chuckled. "I'll be goddamned."

"Sorry," she mumbled.

Suddenly his face brightened with a big smile. "What do you say we get married anyway?"

"Huh?"

"I love you, Lynette. I'm in love with you, and I didn't realize it until right this second."

"Oh, Sid." She shook her head as though she were listening to the ravings of a madman.

"Really," he said. "I've never been happier in my life than I have been the last seven weekends. I've never been more relaxed, more loved for just who I am."

She turned away, unable to look him in the eye.

"Marry me, Lynette. I love you."

She gazed off at the chimneys of the National Paper Factory, then looked back at Sid. "I'm sorry," she said, "but I don't want to marry you. I mean, I like you a lot and we had ourselves some real nice times, that's for sure, but I thought you understood."

He just stood there, blinking rapidly.

"I want to marry a pilot, Sid. I want to live part of my life overseas, the wife of an aviator, Sid."

After a moment he quit blinking, and a looney smile spread across his face. "I believe I'm gettin' the picture." She thought he was going to laugh.

"Damn you!" she screamed. "Goddamn you!" She hurled the engagement ring at him. "Nobody D.O.R.'s after eleven weeks. Nobody!"

He turned away from her, took a few steps, and picked up the ring. He held it up between his thumb and forefinger, then touched it to his forehead as though he was saluting her. He winked and started walking up the road. When he got next to her Falcon he stopped, gave Lynette a look, then jumped in the car, fired it up, and drove away.

"Hey!" She ran down the stairs as the car disappeared around a turn. "Come back!" She shook her fist at nothing. "Come back with my car, you son of a bitch!"

Zack said nothing to Paula on the way to Lynette's, just nodding his head every time she shouted a direction in his ear. They were nearly there when it dawned on him that he didn't know why he was doing this or what he expected to find. What the hell was he going to do if he found big Sid curled up in Lynette's arms? Tell him she was a worthless bitch? Not hardly, Zack thought. Well, the least he could do was make sure everything was okay. If Sid wanted to marry Lynette and have a baby, that was his business. Zack just didn't want him feeling too ashamed to seek out his friends.

"It's up there!" Paula yelled, pointing to a wooden bungalow, in need of a paint job, up the road.

Zack pulled off the road and stopped in front of the house.

"Shit!" Paula said.

"What's wrong?"

Paula gestured toward the empty parking space. "I don't think she's here."

"Great. Maybe they eloped."

"Lynette!" Paula jumped off the Triumph and ran up the steps. "Lynette!" She knocked on the door.

Zack sat on the bike, staring sullenly at Paula, trying not to acknowledge how good she looked.

Paula turned around and gestured to him. "Come on. She's inside."

Zack leaped off the bike and followed Paula into the house. Lynette sat at the kitchen table smoking a Virginia Slim. She did not look like the happiest person on earth.

"You seen Sid?" Paula asked.

Lynette nodded.

"Well, where is he?" Zack said.

Lynette waved her arm back and forth. "Been here and gone. Stole my car too."

"Where'd he go?" Zack demanded.

It was as though Lynette hadn't heard him. "Can you believe it? He D.O.R.'d in the twelfth week. How the hell can you win? I ask you, how..."

"Do you know where he went?" Zack asked.

Lynette shook her head. "But if that car ain't back here by tomorrow, I'm callin' the cops. I mean, there's some..."

Zack grabbed her by the shoulders and forced her to meet his eyes. "What did you tell him about the baby?"

She just stared at him for a moment.

"What?"

"That there isn't one, as of today." Lynette looked away. "I just got my period."

"Oh, Jesus!" Zack shook his head and stared at the floor.

"I couldn't believe it," Lynette said to Paula. "He still wanted to marry me."

"And you turned him down?" Zack said.

"Of course." Lynette lit another Slim from the one in her hand. "I don't want no Okie from Muskogee. I can get that right here in Port Angeles."

"You little bitch!" Zack grabbed her again and began shaking her. "How could you?"

Lynette knocked his hands away. "Easy."

Zack glared at her with hatred in his eyes. "Just answer me this, Lynette. Was there ever a baby?"

She said nothing.

"That's all I want to know. Did you make up that baby, Lynette?"

She shook her head tentatively.

"Did you?!" he bellowed.

She exhaled and looked at the table. "Of course there was a baby. I'd never lie about something like that." She looked up at her fellow deb. "Would I, Paula?"

Paula couldn't answer. Zack looked from her to Lynette and back to Paula again.

"Boy," he said. "You're quite a pair, aren't you?" Then he pushed past Paula and strode out of the house.

Lynette gave Paula a helpless grin.

Paula shook her head. "Did you make it up, Lynette?"

Lynette said nothing, and Paula had her answer. She stepped forward and slapped Lynette across the face with all her might. "God help you, Lynette!" She turned and started out of the house.

"Paula!"

She turned at the doorway. "What?"

"You're no better than me, Paula. You're just the same."

"We both know that's not true." Paula ran from the house, clattered down the steps, hurried over to Zack's motorcycle, and climbed on the back.

"What do you think you're doin'?" He started it up.

"I want to come with you."

"Why?" He revved the engine a couple of times.

"Because he's my friend too."

Zack glanced over his shoulder at her, then faced front and shrugged. She tightened her arms around his waist, and he sped off down the highway.

Every time Sid floored the Falcon, smoke poured out of the exhaust pipe as though the decaying vehicle were on fire. He found the smoke amusing, and he laughed out loud a couple of times before pulling up in front of a liquor store. The brakes squeaked too, and the goddamn wreck was beginning to overheat. Sid slapped the fender as he walked past. "You need work, machine. I believe you're about all washed up."

He bought a fifth of Jack Daniel's, and he took four big gulps before starting up the car and heading down the highway once again. The booze was warm going down, but it made him feel even more giddy and out of control. Tears ran down his cheeks. Maybe he should call Susan. Good old Susan. Yeah, she'd be there for him. She'd always be there for him. He laughed, then scrinched up his face and looked at himself in the mirror. "It's okay, Sid." He mimicked a simpering voice. "Anything y'all did is okay, honey. Oh, Jesus!" He pulled the car off the shoulder, barely avoiding a plunge into the ocean. He glanced at the mirror again. "It don't matter that you're a fucked-up jive-ass fool, honey chile. I'll take you back. I'll always be there for you." He pounded the steering wheel and roared with laughter. He took another long swallow of whiskey, then glanced at the temperature gauge. The needle was resting securely on *H*. He noticed some smoke coming out from under the hood. He took another drink. "Fuck it!" he gasped. "Come on, Bessie Lou!" he hollered at the car. "Only another mile to the Tides Inn Motel!"

He made it to the motel parking lot. He took another swig of whiskey and got out of the car, leaving the keys in the ignition. "Sweet of you to do the same, Lynette," he said. He put his hand on the smoking hood, then pulled back when his flesh began to burn. "Mission accomplished, Bessie Lou. Enjoy your leave." He staggered into the Tides Inn office.

"You're early this week." The man behind the counter gave him a knowing nod.

"Ain't this a bitch?"

The man laughed.

"Have a drink." Sid held out the bottle.

The man patted his stomach. "Can't take it." He pushed a registration form toward Sid.

"Too bad." Sid filled in the form, then dropped some money on the counter.

"Your friend coming?" the man asked, a lecherous twinkle in his eye.

Sid looked at him for a moment, then nodded slowly. "I'm meetin' my friend," he said. "Meetin' my best goddamn friend." He took another pull on the bottle. "Sure you won't have a drink?"

"Thank you, no," the man said.

"Suit yourself." Sid took the key and put it in his pocket, feeling the box that contained the engagement ring. He pulled it out. "Hey."

"What?" the man said.

Sid pulled out the ring and held it up in front of the man's eyes. "You ever see this one?" He laid the ring on his tongue, closed his mouth, and swallowed. It went down smoothly, but he put a little Jack Daniel's on top of it just to make sure. "Give my regards to Broadway." He turned and headed for his room.

Zack was relieved to see the Falcon in front of the Tides Inn, even more so when he pulled up and saw the smoke coming out from under the hood. He cut off the Triumph's engine. "He ain't been here long." He and Paula both got off the bike.

"I'll find out what room he's in." Paula ran to the office, then came out a few seconds later, pointing upstairs. "He's up in seven."

Zack smiled. "His favorite room. Well, maybe he's not too drunk."

They went up to the room and listened for a moment. Some soap opera was going on the television. Zack knocked on the door. "Sid, it's me. Zack."

There was no response.

"Sid! Open up!" Zack pounded on the door again, then turned the knob. The door swung open, but there was nothing in the room but the television blaring idiotically at an empty bottle of Jack Daniel's on the nightstand.

"Sid?" Zack walked into the room, Paula behind him. "Sid!"

Still nothing. The bathroom door was closed, and Zack walked over and tapped on it gently. "Hey, Sid, you on the crapper or something?"

Paula turned off the television, and the silence was eerie.

"Sid?" Zack tried the door, and it opened. He pushed it back slowly, not wanting to surprise his friend in the middle of something embarrassing.

He saw the shoes first, about three feet off the floor, and for a moment he could not force his eyes to look any farther. But then his training took over, and before he could be crushed by the enormity of the situation he had turned the chair on the floor upright, stood on it, and, with some superhuman strength, had ripped Sid's necktie off the drainage pipes and lowered his friend's incredibly heavy body to the bathroom floor. Then he bellowed like some stricken jungle beast. "Why?" he howled. "Why, Sid?" He cradled his friend's body in his arms and rocked him back and forth like a baby. "You stupid fucking Okie! Why did you do it? Why didn't you talk to me first, man?" He sobbed for a moment. "Why didn't you even try?" Then he broke down and wept, barely feeling Paula's hand on his back and barely hearing her cries of dismay.

He stayed with Sid while Paula went to call the police, and after they had come and he had answered all their questions, he slipped away and walked down the beach for a couple of miles. He would have walked for longer, but he reached a point where there was no passage between the sea and the rocks. He tossed stones into the gray water awhile, then turned and trudged slowly back to the motel. He didn't think about Sid, but about what a stupid cheat life was, how nothing ever worked out the way you planned, and how you got the shaft no matter which way you turned. He didn't even think about what he was going to do now. A jet roared by overhead, and it gave him no inspiration. He might have walked completely past the motel if Paula hadn't walked down to the surf to meet him.

"Hi," she said.

He nodded, thinking how stupid words were. How could anyone say "hi" after what had happened?

"Everything's taken care of," Paula said. "I spoke to the chaplain at the base, and he's gonna call Sid's folks."

He barely heard her.

"Zack?"

"I came in the back door the way I always did." He began to walk slowly, pantomiming gestures. "I went straight for the refrigerator." He shook his head. "No milk. No peanut butter." He turned and met Paula's eye. "She was the worst when it came to shopping. I had to do it all myself." He walked a few more steps, then stopped. "I went to get some money off her to go to the store, and I found her in the bathroom. She was lying in her own throw-up, and I thought, Goddamn it! Now I gotta spend my afternoon cleaning up the place." He looked down at a large stone in the sand at his feet. "Ma! Hey, get up!" He stared for a moment, then shook his head.

"Zack, you..."

"But her face was a, uh, a funny color, and there was a bottle lying there. There was one little speckled pill stuck to the top." His voice trailed off, and he gave a little laugh.

Paula came to him and put her hand on his shoulder, but he jerked away as though she were trying to hurt him.

"Don't!" he commanded, and moved off down the beach.

She followed him, a couple of paces behind. "Zack, don't do this to yourself. You didn't kill your mom and you didn't kill Sid. They did it to themselves."

"Thank you." He took off his hat and hurled it into the water.

"Zack, there was nothing you could've done."

He stopped, reached in his pocket, and pulled out some money. He offered it to her. "Here. Go get a cab or something."

"Why?"

"'Cause I don't want to talk to you!"

She shook her head.

"Have it your way." He dropped the money at her feet, then started up to the parking lot and his motorcycle.

"That's not fair!" she yelled, running after him. "You're not the only one who's feeling awful right now. What if..."

He turned at the top of the hill. "What if what?"

"What if I were a part of what happened today?"

He shook his head. "I don't get you, woman."

"I knew Lynette was thinking of trapping him. I could have said something to you."

"But you didn't."

She nodded. "But I didn't."

He put out his hand as though it was nothing. "Hey, don't worry about it. New class'll be along soon, and you and Lynette'll be right back in business." He sneered at her with contempt.

"I don't deserve that," Paula said. "I never lied to you. I'm not Lynette!" She wiped the tears out of her eyes. "I love you, goddamnit! I loved you from the first time I saw you!"

He dropped his eyes, then turned and sprinted to his motorcycle. He did not look back at her as he raced down the highway.

He parked the Triumph by the barracks and took a long look down the company street to where Foley stood in front of the remaining candidates. Sorry bastards, Zack thought. What the hell was it all worth, anyway? He couldn't de-

cide who had the most blame for Sid's death,
Lynette or the program with all its silly bullshit
codes and tests of character. Maybe they were
connected, some kind of diabolical conspiracy
to drive a man out of his tree.

Zack started down the street toward the formation. His tie was loose, and the top button
of his shirt was undone. His jacket was open,
and his pants were a mess. Fuck it, he thought.
They couldn't do a thing to him. He had no idea
what he was going to do now. Maybe he'd
D.O.R., then go kill Lynette. Pretty simple.
Then he and Byron could get a couple of teenage
girls and lay up with them until the cops came
and took him away. What a way to go.

Foley turned the formation, and they began
marching toward Zack. Then he halted them.
"Mayo," Foley said, "the rest of your class
knows about Candidate Worley. We're all very
sorry."

Zack eyed him for a moment. "Sir, this officer
candidate requests permission to speak to you
in private."

Foley glanced at the formation, then back at
Zack. "I'm busy, Mayo. It'll have to wait."

For sure, Zack thought. Nothing gets in the
way of the fucking program. "It's important,
sir!" More important than marching these dip-
shits around.

"You didn't hear me, Mayo. I said I'm busy.
And so are you!"

"Say what?"

"Look at yourself. You're a mess. Go get
cleaned up!"

Zack almost started laughing. "I don't need this," he said.

"What?" Foley gave him a hard look.

"I said I don't need this." Then he pointed his finger at Foley. "And I don't need you and I don't need the Navy!" He dismissed it all with a single gesture and started off down the street. "I don't need anybody," he muttered.

"Mayo!" Foley bellowed.

He turned and smiled at the D.I., walking backward for a few steps.

"You want to meet me in private, Mayo? You got it."

Zack stopped moving.

Foley pointed off to the right. "The blimp hangar. Now!"

Zack gave him a questioning look.

"Move it!" Foley bellowed.

"You move it!" Zack began striding toward the old building. "Move!"

Foley quick-marched ahead of him, and Zack stared at his back, full of hatred and rage. This was it. This was perfect. He was going to kick the living shit out of this chump, humiliate him in front of the remaining candidates, whose respect he had grudgingly won. Zack looked over his shoulder as his classmates fell in tentatively behind him. They didn't know whether to follow or hang back. Zack didn't give a damn, and he figured Foley didn't either. They were going to know who won anyway; the humiliation for the loser would be the same as if they had watched.

Ahead of him, Foley took off his tie and put it in his shirt pocket. Zack pulled his off and stuffed it in his jacket. Foley pulled his shirt out of his pants and began unbuttoning it. Zack took off his coat, held it under one arm, and undid his shirt. He walked into the blimp hangar a few feet behind his D.I., and both men tossed their clothes off to the side. Foley sat down on the edge of the mat and pulled off his shoes and socks. Zack sat on the floor and did the same. Then Foley jumped up on the mat, walked to the middle, and folded his arms over his chest. He was ready.

Zack glanced over his shoulder once again. His classmates seemed afraid to enter the building. A couple of them were hanging back by the doors, and the others were taking up positions at the many cracks and crevices in the obsolete building. Well, Zack hoped they got their eyes full. Probably some of them would be happy to see Foley whip his ass. In a few minutes they'll know. He turned and jumped up on the mat, meeting Foley's relentless gaze. There wasn't any need to talk; they both knew the rules, or the rule: there wasn't one; this was all out. Zack had not forgotten his lesson from the alley in Olongapo.

Almost without thinking, Zack whirled and caught Foley in the mouth with a spinning crescent kick. He hit the stunned sergeant with a left jab and a right cross, then dropped him to the mat with another spinning kick to the chin.

Foley rolled to his side and came up on his feet looking wobbly. He seemed about to topple to his left, and Zack swung another kick to help send him on his way. But Foley straightened up suddenly, caught Zack's foot in his hand, and sent him flying halfway across the mat. Zack landed with his back to Foley, and as he turned he caught a foot in the face. He bellowed with pain, but kept his body moving, rolling and getting to his feet once again.

He and Foley both assumed boxing stances. They were both breathing heavily and took a couple of moments for rest. Then Foley advanced. Zack faked for his head and punched him in the stomach. It felt as if he had hit a steel door. Zack moved his head in time to miss a jab, but Foley moved in close and got a foot behind him and pushed him over on his back. Zack rolled, lessening the force of the kick to his back, then came up as Foley charged. In an instant he knew he had the fight won. He leaped back to avoid Foley's crescent kick, then moved in as Foley came around. Zack smashed his face with a left, and Foley suddenly stopped as though he were playing a child's game and had been commanded to freeze. Zack hit him again with a right, and blood spurted from Foley's nostrils. The D.I. brought his arms up slowly, too slowly to avoid Zack's kick to the side of his face, then toppled like a statue that had been knocked off its pedestal. Zack spit out a gob of blood before advancing on the sergeant. One more kick to the head. A coup de grace, so to speak.

Foley's eyes opened as Zack cocked his leg, and his kick was halfway home before Foley's foot smashed into his groin like an artillery shell that seemed to explode within his body.

Zack's foot never got to Foley. The D.I. rolled out of the way and stood up as Zack, howling in agony, turned ninety degrees and crumpled to the mat where he covered his balls with his hand.

Foley looked at him for a moment. "More?"

Zack shook his head.

"Now you do whatever you want to do." Foley bowed formally to him, then walked off the mat. He was shaky, but Zack thought he was doing an admirable job of covering it up.

11

Zack closed his eyes and lay on the mat for a long while, thinking vaguely about what he should do and almost dozing off a couple of times. Maybe the best thing would be for him to leave, to go turn in his D.O.R., get on his Triumph and go. He felt so tired that he didn't see how he could get up for even another week of the program. How could he face Foley again? And how could he sort out the business with Sid?

He heard some shuffling on the floor and opened his eyes to see Perryman, Seeger, and Della Serra standing there. He felt a sudden surge of strong emotion, and his eyes misted over. He rubbed them with his thumb and forefinger, then buried his face in his arm until he had regained control. Finally he opened his eyes and sat up, realizing that the people before him were the three best friends he had on earth. After a moment he forced a smile.

"You okay?" Perryman asked.

"Never better." Zack moved a bit and groaned. His nuts were going to ache for a while.

"That was something," Della Serra said.

Zack nodded. "I didn't want to beat him in front of you all."

"Sure," Seeger said.

"You know," Zack said, "it wouldn't be good to undermine his position of authority."

"You're all heart," Perryman said. "Now what do you say we go get cleaned up?"

Zack nodded and got to his feet. "I might have to walk a little slower than usual."

Casey elbowed him. "Maybe we could go horseback riding later."

He winced at the thought of it, then the four of them headed for the barracks. "Thanks, you guys," he said.

He was feeling pretty good by the time he got back to his room, but the sight of Sid's empty locker and the rolled mattress on his bunk set him off again. Perryman patted him on the back. "I'm sorry, man," he said, then lay down on his bunk and left Zack with his own thoughts.

Zack stood in front of his locker for a moment, once again unsure of what to do. He got past the surge of rage at Foley and Lynette, but he somehow still couldn't see himself staying in the program, wearing all that white and gold on graduation day. But where else would you go? he finally asked himself. *Where the hell else would you go?*

He caught a glance of himself in his little mirror. His face was a mass of bruises caked with blood. Plug ugly, he thought. Well, even if he was going to D.O.R., he would have to take a shower and change his clothes first. He grabbed some things out of his locker. "I'm goin' to get pretty," he said to Perryman.

Perryman sat up and looked at him. "That'll take some doing."

"I reckon." Zack trudged down the hall, and soon lost himself in the steam and hot water of the shower.

He had always thought it was bad to make decisions on an empty stomach, so after he got cleaned up and changed he went over to the snack bar and ate the largest hamburger they had and chased it with a ham-and-cheese sandwich. He had not eaten since before sunrise, and the food did wonders for his mental attitude. He took a little walk up by the officers club, where he leaned against a tree and watched the young flyboys and instructors go in and out with their wives and their dates. Their debs, he thought, wondering what Paula and Lynette were doing tonight. Maybe they'd even stay away from the base until his class had left. Don't be bitter, he told himself. He shook his head almost involuntarily as the thought came into his brain that Sid should have known better. Christ, it was true, so why the hell hadn't he? That was a mystery he wasn't prepared to deal with. Not yet, anyway. He headed on back to the barracks.

He stopped by the phone next to the orderly room, threw in some change, and made his call. When the gruff voice came on the line, Zack said, "Byron?"

"Yeah?"

"It's Zack."

There was a moment of silence, then Byron said, "Zackie. Hey, pard, how are you?"

"I'm fine," Zack said.

"Hey, you don't need money, do you?"

"Not really."

"What's happening?" Zack could hear someone else rustling around in Byron's room. Maybe he even had a couple of them with him.

"You doin' anything weekend after next?" Zack asked.

"Nothin' I ain't done every weekend for the last thirty years."

The guy was consistent, you had to give him that. "How about comin' over to my graduation?"

"Your graduation?"

"I think I'm gonna make it, Pop."

After a moment Byron said, "Well, I'll be goddamned."

"It's actually on Friday, so you won't have to miss a whole lot."

"I'd pass up a three-day liberty to see you graduate. That's great, pard. Really great."

"See you there." Zack hung up and stood in the hallway for a moment. Then he ran up the stairs two at a time. Christ, if he was going to stay in the program he'd better get his boonies shined up for tomorrow.

* * *

As she had every morning since Sid had killed himself, Paula awoke before her alarm went off. She tiptoed across the room and pushed in the button on the clock, careful not to wake her little sisters. The alarm was set for six-thirty, and it still wasn't even six. She went in the bathroom, washed her face and got dressed for work, then went to the kitchen and started the coffee. She liked being up before everyone else. The house was still and peaceful, without the emotional tension that hung in the air when everyone was awake.

On the front porch, she sat on the top step and lit a cigarette. Sid had been dead about ten days now, and Paula and Lynette had scarcely spoken during that time. Paula had resigned from the world of the Puget debs. She had resolved never to return to the base again, not with Lynette, not at the request of Nellie Rufferwell, not because some horny flight candidate or officer asked her. That part of her life was over, and as soon as she could get a little more money together she would be leaving town and beginning her new life. The last weekend she had gone over to Seattle and spent Saturday in the library, looking up information on junior colleges and trying to figure out where she would go. She had pretty much made up her mind to stay in Seattle, although her more adventuresome side kept urging her to go to San Francisco or Los Angeles. She could worry about that later. She figured she would have the money by the end of the year. She wouldn't have to make up her mind until then.

She heard her parents' alarm go off. "Here we go," she muttered. Things actually hadn't been that bad around the house lately, but Paula knew she had to go, more to get on with her new life than to escape the old. She wanted to be away from the factory and the town where her reputation as a deb would be hard to live down. She'd probably even like her parents more once she got established on her own. Meanwhile, there was the routine to be gotten through.

The worst part of the routine now was the car pool to work. She and her mother usually rode with Bunny, and Bunny loved nothing more than mean-spirited gossip. She had been full of questions and speculations about Sid's suicide, and Paula had finally told her that she didn't want to hear anything more about it. For Bunny it seemed to be nothing more than an interesting piece of news, something to pick over, the way a vulture would a new carcass until there was nothing left. Painful as the experience had been for Paula, keeping the pain was more important than gossiping about it until you couldn't feel anything anymore. Paula kept to herself on the rides to and from work, listening to her mother and Bunny, and making resolutions on how she would not conduct her life.

Once she was at work, things weren't so bad, although today Lynette fell in behind her in the line for the time clock and gave her a friendly smile. "Hi, Paula."

"How you doin', Lynette?"

"Fine." Lynette had seemed to recover quickly from the news about Sid. Sometimes Paula thought it hadn't bothered her at all, and that if it hadn't been for the inconvenience of having her car stolen and the radiator ruined, Lynette would have forgotten about it the next day.

Lynette nudged her and gestured with her head toward the inside of the factory. "What do you think of the new mechanics?"

Paula looked at them and saw nothing she would be interested in. "Great, Lynette." She pulled out her card and punched herself in. "You know what today is?"

"Friday, thank God." Lynette punched in too.

"It's graduation day."

"Oh, yeah," Lynette said.

"Hope he made it."

Lynette shrugged and headed off to her position on the conveyor belt.

Paula went through the day's drudgery like a robot, often thinking about Zack, but knowing she would never see him again. She guessed he had probably stayed in the program, although hotheaded as he was, he could be in Timbuktu by now. But she preferred to think of him graduating, finishing flight school and getting jets, then flying around the world. She wondered what kind of girl he would finally marry, but the thought made her sad, so she would think about him as a bachelor, although the older he got the sadder that would get too. Sometimes she felt angry over the way he had treated her, but she did her best to remember the good times they had shared.

"Eyes, right!" Foley commanded, and the twenty-one surviving members of his officer candidate class turned their heads toward the bleachers. "Present, arms!" The group saluted, and the gesture was returned by the commanding officer and his minions from the dais where they stood. "Order, arms!" The candidates lowered their arms to the side. "Eyes, front!" Their heads snapped to the front.

It was a nearly perfect day, the sun high above in a clear blue sky, a slight breeze fluttering the greenery at the edge of the parade field and keeping the temperature in the high seventies. The precise cadence of the marching band sent chills down Zack's spine. Christ, he had really made it! With just a few minutes remaining until he received his commission, there wasn't much he could do to screw up. Even Byron was in the bleachers, applauding like a madman for his son.

Foley marched them past the bleachers, turned them left, then left again, then left another time, halting them in front of the bleachers and leaving them at rigid attention. After a few remarks, the commanding officer led them through their commissioning oath, and although Zack could feel his face turn red, he kept his voice from cracking all the way through:

I do solemnly swear that I will support and defend the Constitution of the United States of America against all enemies foreign and domestic, that I will bear true faith and allegiance to the same, that I take this obligation freely, without any mental reservation or purpose of evasion, and that I will well and faithfully discharge the duties of the office on which I am about to enter. So help me God.

The commander looked them over for a moment, a slight smile creasing his crusty face. "I hereby commission you ensigns in the United States Navy. Congratulations. Dismissed!"

The new officers tossed their hats into the air and let go with a collective cheer of exultation and relief. Zack hugged Casey, then Perryman and Della Serra. They would talk later; right now there was more pressing business.

Family and friends poured out of the bleachers, and soon each officer was surrounded by well-wishers. Byron approached Zack with a proud smile on his face. His uniform was perfectly cleaned and pressed, his face was clean-shaven, and even his eyes were clear. He must have stayed sober last night, Zack thought. "Hey, pard!" Byron said.

Zack showed him a piece of paper in his pocket.

"What's that?"

"My orders to Pensacola for basic flight training; then it's on to jets."

"My son the flyboy."

"You got it." He handed Byron his ensign's shoulder boards.

Byron looked at them for a moment, and tears actually formed in his eyes. He looked away from his son, then turned back and began buttoning the boards on Zack's shoulders. "You know, I didn't think you'd make it."

Zack nodded.

"I wanted you to and all, but..." His voice trailed off.

"I know, Pop," Zack said.

Byron buttoned on the second board, took a step backward, and slapped Zack on the arm. "So, you must be pretty damn proud right now."

Zack shrugged. "I feel okay."

"Don't give me that," Byron said. "You feel like a million bucks, and you should. You're bursting with it."

Zack smiled at his father. "Okay, I'm feeling pretty good. But don't expect any of that patriotic bullshit out of me."

"Not from you, pard. Not now anyway. That's something you catch, like the clap, if you stay in a few years."

They both laughed, then just stood there staring at each other.

"Well," Byron said, "you'd better get your butt over to your D.I. and give him that silver dollar you got in your pocket. Otherwise I'm gonna give you your first salute right now."

Zack shook his head as he was hit by a sudden wave of emotion. "Yes, sir!" He turned on his heel and walked smartly toward Foley.

The D.I., hardass to the end, stood off to the

side of the bleachers, his swagger stick in his hand, his face set like a stone, receiving his worms, scuzzes, and college pukes. Zack watched as Perryman stood at attention in front of the D.I. Foley saluted him, Perryman saluted back, then handed the sergeant a silver dollar. Tradition! The first tradition. Casey stepped up and saluted. Foley returned the gesture. "Congratulations, Ensign Seeger, sir!"

"Thank you, sir," she said. "I mean, Sergeant." She handed him the dollar and hurried back to her family.

Zack stepped up, but was unable to look at Foley for a moment.

"Congratulations, Ensign Mayo, sir!"

When Zack looked up, Foley was locked in a perfect salute. Zack returned the gesture, tears coming to his eyes. "I'll never forget you as long as I live, Sergeant."

"I know," Foley said.

Zack dug in his pocket, pulled out the silver dollar, and handed it to Foley. "I want you to know that I never would've made it without you."

Foley's eyes misted over. "Thank you, sir." He looked away.

"Well, good-bye." He reached out and shook Foley's hand.

"See you in the fleet, sir!" Foley snapped off a second salute.

"Yeah." Zack saluted back. "See you in the fleet, Sarge. And thank you."

Foley grinned and shook his head.

Zack backed off a few steps, spun on his heel, and walked away.

Zack said good-bye to Byron, who was shipping out to Hawaii the next day, then watched Seeger and Della Serra as they drove off with their families. They would all be together at Pensacola in two weeks, beginning another segment of their training. He headed back to the barracks and found Perryman in their room, just packing the last of his things. "Nice goin', Ensign," Zack said.

"Hey, Zack. Never thought we'd get this far, huh?"

"Well," Zack shrugged. "I had my doubts about you, but..." They both guffawed and clapped each other on the back.

"Where you headin'?" Zack asked.

"St. Louis. My wife's got family there."

"Sounds good."

"Be nice to have a break," Perryman said. "But this stuff's in my bones now. I'm actually looking forward to Pensacola." He closed up his duffel bag and snapped it shut. "Where you goin', man?"

Zack shrugged. "Still tryin' to make up my mind." He stared pensively out the window.

Perryman shouldered his bag. "Hey?"

"Hm?" Zack turned and looked at him.

"She always seemed like a pretty good woman to me. I mean, what've you got to lose by seein' her again?"

Zack eyed him for a moment, then surveyed the room with its shined floor, its empty bunks with rolled mattresses, its empty lockers. Just some loneliness, he thought.

"Thanks, man," Zack said.

"See you in Pensacola." Perryman started out of the room.

"Into the wild blue yonder," Zack said.

He packed his bag, then sat on the edge of his bunk for a few minutes, time to remember Sid. "I made it, hoss," he muttered. He resolved not to forget Sid's part in getting him through. He probably wouldn't have a friend like that for quite a while. "So long," he said as he stood up. He hoisted up his bag and walked out of the empty barracks.

As he strapped the bag on the back of the Triumph, he noticed a group of thirty or so civilians lined up by the orderly room, Foley walking up and down in front of them, looking at the new candidates as though they were the scum of the earth. "I don't believe what I'm seein'," Foley bellowed. "Look at all that hair! All those lard bellies from junk food and pot! Where you been all your lives, at an orgy? Listening to Mick Jagger and bad-mouthing your country, I bet."

As the new class burst out laughing, Zack started the Triumph and headed down the street toward the formation. When he came abreast of the new candidates, he stopped, allowing the bike to idle softly about ten feet behind Foley. The D.I. had called out a big boy with long hair.

"What's your name, boy?"

"Campbell, sir!"

"Where you from, Campbell?"

"Texas, sir. Amarillo."

"Texas? Only things come out of Texas are steers and queers. I don't see no horns on you so you must be a queer, boy."

"No, sir!" Campbell bellowed.

Zack knew that Foley wasn't going to turn around. He revved the bike a couple of times, kicked it into gear, and sped off the base, heading toward the ferry to Port Angeles.

As Zack strode into the paper mill, he caught a glimpse of himself in the mirror by the locker room. He *did* look good, he thought, with his perfect white uniform and his ensign's gold. A few of the women on the paper-towel line looked up at him; two of them even smiled. But he kept his face set sternly. Hell, he was here on an important mission. And he wasn't going to ask anybody where she was. He would just keep looking until he found her.

He found Esther Pokrifki first. She glanced up from the napkin line, her face dull and uncomprehending for a moment. Then she seemed to gasp—Zack couldn't hear over the sound of all the machinery—and the back of her hand went up to her mouth. Zack nodded at her, but kept on walking.

He didn't want to see Lynette, but he settled for not having to face her. He recognized her from behind, but barely broke stride as he walked past her, and when she said "Zack?" he didn't bother to turn around. He had spied

Paula stacking bags in the distance, and he went straight toward her.

She put one pile of bags on top of another, and watched for a second as they moved down the conveyor belt. The flash of white and gold was incongruous, but it barely registered, and she turned away to grab another pile of bags. Suddenly she stood up straight, turned off the conveyor, and faced Zack as he stopped two feet away from her. Something was wrong, and she didn't know what. "Zack?"

"In the flesh." He grinned. "Hi."

She took off the corduroy cap she was wearing and shook out her hair. "Hi." She pointed at the shoulder boards. "You made it."

He nodded. "I made it."

"Congratulations." She grinned and gave him a little salute.

"Oh, Christ," he said.

"What?"

He shrugged.

"So you're off to Florida?" She looked around nervously at all the people watching them.

"I was just about to leave. But then I realized I was forgetting something." He too surveyed the staring women. "And then I knew that if I forgot it my life would never get right."

She gave him a questioning look.

"Will you go with me, Paula?"

She bit her lip and looked down at the floor, then she nodded a couple of times.

"Thanks." He stepped forward and kissed the tears off her cheeks, then he lifted her into his arms.

"Hey," she said. "What're you doin'?"

He smiled. "No use wasting time. We're goin'."

She pulled his face to her and kissed it hard. A couple of women applauded, and a few more joined in. "Let's go," she said.

He began walking toward the exit. It felt so good to hold her again that he never wanted to let go.

"Way to go, Paula!"

Zack looked over his shoulder to see Lynette smiling through her tears at her friend.

"Way to go!"

Zack carried her out into the sunshine and kissed her again. "I don't think I'll ever get enough of you," he said.

"I'll do my best to make sure you don't."

"Oh, man." He rested his cheek against hers. "This is the greatest day of my life."

"Mine too," she said.

The National Bestseller by
GARY JENNINGS

"A blockbuster historical novel. . . . From the start of this epic, the reader is caught up in the sweep and grandeur, the richness and humanity of this fictive unfolding of life in Mexico before the Spanish conquest. . . . Anyone who lusts for adventure, or that book you can't put down, will glory in AZTEC!"

The Los Angeles Times

"A dazzling and hypnotic historical novel. . . . AZTEC has everything that makes a story appealing . . . both ecstasy and appalling tragedy . . . sex . . . violence . . . and the story is filled with revenge. . . . Mr. Jennings is an absolutely marvelous yarnspinner. . . . A book to get lost in!"

The New York Times

"Sumptuously detailed. . . . AZTEC falls into the same genre of historical novel as SHOGUN."

Chicago Tribune

"Unforgettable images. . . . Jennings is a master at graphic description. . . . The book is so vivid that this reviewer had the novel experience of dreaming of the Aztec world, in technicolor, for several nights in a row . . . so real that the tragedy of the Spanish conquest is truly felt."

Chicago Sun Times

AVON Paperback   **55889 . . . $3.95**